LUST

Love is Cure, Vol. 1 - Vices & Virtues Series

Book Two

Brookelyn Mosley

More By Brookelyn Mosley

Links to the below stories can be found here (https://brookelynmosley.com/ebooks-paperbacks/)

Novels/Novellas/Novelettes/Series

- No Fraternizing, Pt. 1
- No Fraternizing, Pt. 2
- No Fraternizing, Pt. 3
- First Came Love: The Love, Hate & Revenge Prequel
- Love, Hate & Revenge, Pt. 1
- Love, Hate & Revenge, Pt. 2
- Love, Hate & Revenge, Pt. 3
- Girl Code
- Mr. & Mrs. Jones
- Forbidden: An Anthology
- They Call Me Mello
- A Love Deferred
- Indecent Arrangement
- Last Comes Love
- Ebb & Flow
- PRIDE
- Meant To Be
- LUST
- Loveless
- GREED
- Rekindled
- My First, My Last

ByBK Exclusives

Bed Bully
Stuck
LHR Rewind Series
Home Before Midnight
Maybe This Time Will Be Different
Lovekilla
Incoming Call
Rough
WYD
Drinks on Me
Cali & Lee
Ray & Jay
Living Out a Love Song
Glimpses
One Mic
With Love, Ayanna & Dallas
Just Friends
Lena's Ex-File
Dream Boss
Chateau Luxure

Click Here to see if new exclusive shorts have been added to ByBK
(Copy + paste this link if the above link doesn't work: https://
bybrookelynmosley.com/collections/ebooks)

ACKNOWLEDGMENTS

A loving thank you to my amazing husband who is without a doubt one of my biggest supporters. Your support is worth its weight in gold. A special thank you to my reading family. To the active members in my Facebook reading group, my beloved beta readers for this project, and my supporters across all social medias. You all have embraced my brand of writing and I'm beyond appreciative of it. Shout out to the readers who have reached out to me to share your thoughts regarding my books. I thank you for keeping me motivated and excited to create new projects for you. When I write, I keep you in mind. Thank you for your support. It's my soul food.

Message From The Author

Thank you for downloading book two in the *Love Is Cure, Vol. 1 – Vices & Virtues* series. This series was definitely a labor of love to brainstorm and create, and I'm happy I get to share it with you. Book two like all the books in the series plays matchmaker with the vices & virtues a.k.a. the sinners and the saints. In book one, we watched what happened when pride (the sin) and humility (the virtue) paired up and love cured all. We'll do the same with *LUST*, witnessing what happens when lust and chastity cross paths once again. Book one and book two are both stand-alone like all the books in this series. You can read them in whatever order you choose but if you are reading them as I release them then you are reading them in the ideal order. *LUST*, like most of the books in the *LIC* series, contains explicit sexual content and adult language. If you are sensitive to the aforementioned, this may not be the reading experience for you. If you've gotten this far, thanks for reading and thank you in advance for investing your time in flipping through *LUST*. Enjoy the ride.

Love,
Brookelyn.

Dedicated to the saints and the sinners...

ONE
MANHATTAN, JULY 5, 2019

LEELAH

"So, Leelah, what's your sign?"

I rolled my eyes away from my glass and up at him to see an annoying grin stretching his lips. His name was Marshall, but in my mind I'd given him the name Martian because of his spaceships for eyes he kept landing in my cleavage.

It wasn't *him* that annoyed me, per se. It was more so his type. White-collar nerd. Very much *not* my type. Not that my preference was any better. If anything, I would consider Marshall to be a step above the rest.

I sighed at that fact while wrapping my hand tight around the bowl of my wineglass.

"She's a Cancer," my sister Gena said beside me.

She combed her fingers through her curls she cut into a cute asymmetrical style and that she dyed a honey brown earlier that week. Gena was so nervous and I couldn't understand why. Our dates were lames. What's to be nervous about?

This was her idea, this blind date. It was a double-blind date, actually. She met this guy on this dating app and he had a friend, Marshall, the white-collar nerd. To make things less awkward between her and her dating app find, she invited *me*, her little sister, to accompany her on this train wreck.

"And she loves moons," Gena bragged. "She's obsessed with them! She has a tattoo of the moon cycles. They wrap around her ankle with the last phase stopping at her foot."

I stared at her from the side of my eye and she tucked her lips in her mouth to keep from laughing.

"And she's in love with stars." She grabbed my wrist and held up my hand. "See?" Gena gestured at the scatter of tiny black stars tatted along the webbing between my index and thumb fingers.

"Oh, that's cool," Marshall said. "Moons and stars are cool. Your hair is cool too, Leelah."

I switched my eyes over to him.

"It's so bouncy, long, and curly. Just unapologetically wild! I *love* that. Reminds me of Chaka Khan's hair." He cheesed. "I like the color too. That brown and blonde suits you so well."

He tried *so* hard. With not even a pinch of flavor.

Dammit.

Mr. Bland was completely in his head and nervous. Sweat beads gathered at his temples and he wouldn't stop bouncing his leg under our table. Marshall only needed to pump his knee just a tad harder to shoot from his seat and rocket into outer space to see in person the moon and stars Gena blabbed about. If there was one thing I couldn't stand, it was an outwardly nervous man.

I wished he'd man the fuck up already.

"Thanks." I strained a smile.

"What about you Gena," her date, Fenton, queried. "What's your sign?"

"Oh my God," I mumbled to myself. "How much more of this must I endure?"

Fenton was less awkward. Handsome, if you liked the generic black ken doll type. You know the one, the kind of doll you find at the dollar store wrapped in cellophane.

"I'm a Libra," Gena answered.

"Oh, the lover of romance," Fenton replied. I'm sure his smile was visible from three city blocks away.

We all hung out at the *Purple Cat*, a bar so small, if you ambled from one end of the room to the next, that would conclude your tour of the joint. It was dark under their roof, with violet lighting searing overhead. There were a few red, white and blue balloons and matching decorations still hanging around since the 4th of July was the day before. Something sticky covered our table. The aforementioned bar detail was par for the course, and so were the patrons who came from all walks of life. From the 9-5ers to the habitual drunks. People crowded the place to capacity. All the makings of an establishment I wouldn't bother being in on a Friday night, but here I was, with my big sister playing wing-woman for flavorless dweebs.

I leaned over in my seat and close to her ear. "Can you *please* go in the back and fuck Fenton so I can leave already? I'm begging you. This is me begging."

Gena snorted a laugh before lifting her glass to her lips.

"So... a psychotherapist," Marshall spoke again. I shut my eyes to keep from rolling them. "How's that job?"

I leaned back in my seat and tossed my hair over my shoulders while taking a deep breath.

"It's not a *job*, it's a career," I replied. "And it's selfless and rewarding."

Marshall nodded quickly. "Oh. Right. Of course."

My eyes moved around us, falling on the faces that made up my night. A couple in one corner kept their lips busy in a lip-lock. They were so engaging, I couldn't help but to stare. It had been two years since I'd experienced even just that. I put myself on an intimacy diet a.k.a. chastity on my 30th birthday once I realized using sex for over a decade to supplement a broken heart was a juvenile idea, a detrimental one actually. Why is 30 the year we all want to get our shit together, anyway?

Two years later, here I sat, needing sex and bad...

"You've been nursing that glass for a while," Marshall pointed out across from me, pulling my attention back on him. "Did you want something else, perhaps?"

... just not with this guy.

I peeked down at my more than half-full glass and shrugged. "No.

I'm not that much in a drinking mood tonight, Martian. I mean Marshall."

Gena choked back a laugh.

"We should order shots," Fenton suggested, his eyes on my sister.

"Oh that's unnecessary." Gena smiled. "I think we're good."

"Pryce Williams is making headlines tonight," the anchor's voice boomed from the overhead speakers, "and it's all centered on New York City and the *Bronx Ballers*."

The mere mention of his name faltered the rhythm of my heart. I snatched my eyes away from our table and focused them up at the flat screen mounted to the bar's wall airing the ten o'clock news.

The brunette anchor added, "Rumors are circulating in his camp that the *Oakland Flames'* center is strongly considering playing for the *Bronx Ballers* in the upcoming basketball season."

"Oh, fuck yeah!" Gena exclaimed. "Yes, yes, *yessss!*"

I whipped my head in her direction and she immediately ditched the smile.

"I mean... that fucking asshole," she spat through her teeth. Gena tucked her lips into her mouth and held back a scream still audible to me.

I forced my view back on the screen.

"Pryce's two season contract with the *Flames* expired on the 1st at midnight, officially making the nine-time All-Star Defensive player an unrestricted free agent, *free* to sign with whatever team he chooses. And according to insiders, he has his sights set on the *Bronx Ballers*."

For what?!

"Is he crazy? Fenton asked across from us. "Why the hell would he leave a championship-winning team for the likes of the *Bronx Ballers*?"

Yeah, why would he do that?

"Right?" Marshall chimed in. "They haven't won a ring since Lennox Walker played for them years ago. And before then it had been a decade since the *Ballers* made it to even the finals."

"Hey, be careful, now!" Gena warned, pointing at them. "Y'all better watch your mouths when you discuss my *Ballers* in front of me. I don't want to have to cut you for my favorite team in the league. Struggling or not."

Fenton threw his hands up in supplication while Marshall chuckled.

While the news did the job of breaking the awkward ice that hovered over our table, my heart was pounding so hard I could hear nothing else besides the news concerning Pryce. That info played on repeat in my brain long after the news anchors transitioned to their next story.

On impulse, I lifted my wineglass to my lips and chugged all the wine left in the bowl.

Everyone at the table grew quiet instantly.

"La, take it easy," Gena whispered beside me, moving in closer to my ear. "Why does even the mention of Pryce's name do this to you *every* time?"

But I ignored her and her question, didn't stop chugging until the glass was empty and I slammed the stem's bottom on the table below me.

"Uh, Fenton?" I called, out of breath and licking my lips of the wine that didn't make it into my mouth, "I'll take those shots now, please."

Two

The bass from the song playing rumbled from the floor speakers five feet from me. The music penetrated the planks of hardwood beneath my feet and sent a soft hum up the legs on the gold-studded pewter couch I relaxed on. The room was foggy with white smoke, but through my haze the three empty champagne bottles sprawled across the floor were visible.

Soft hands skated down my chest, gliding over my pecs. I lolled my head over the neck of the couch and made her my focus. Her long bone straight black sew-in curtained her face as she honed her eyes on me overhead. An innocent grin pulled at her red-painted lips before she drew the bottom one into her mouth and bit down on it.

Below me, another set of hands started their journey up my thighs, stopping at my gray boxers. The owner of those hands hooked her fingers around the band of my underwear, which she used to tug down. I lifted just enough to help her get them off, then glanced down at her.

She licked her lips at the sight of my dick once the muscle sprang out, then she aimed her pupils up at me.

"*Mmm*, I see the big dick rumors were true. Let's see if it tastes as good as it looks though." She leaned in, lapping her pink tongue between the slit of my dickhead, causing my eyes to become slits beneath my brows. The vixen on her knees was lighter than the ebony sister over my shoulder. Her hair was shorter than the beauty above me, too. She wore a tapered cut dyed a gradient of navy blue that almost shone under the lights as black.

I brought the lit blunt I held in the pinch of my index and thumb fingers to my lips and puffed slowly, blowing the smoke up overhead.

It was my final night in Cali, what I hoped to be my final night. Set to fly out to New York in a few hours, I prayed I didn't have to return to this place.

The plan that night was to host a party at a nearby nightclub. The owner insisted I be there, even offered a nice stipend including transportation to and from the event. Who stupid enough would turn down that offer? Not me. So I attended. Turning down the offer of pussy seemed stupid too, so I agreed to that as well.

I found these two at the club. They were throwing me looks all night in VIP. Internet models, both of them were different in terms of preference. Short haircut was petite while black and long had so much ass in her tight yellow dress, when she pranced by me earlier at the club, her cheeks clapped. I couldn't decide which one I wanted to escort back to the hotel, so I invited them both.

Wet warmth covered me from the head of my dick to the root of my shaft. I peeked down to catch shorty with the short haircut playing a disappearing act with my dick using only her mouth.

Head was something I always coveted. My next-door neighbor, Renee, introduced me to this decadent brand of pleasure in my teens. She hooked me the moment she flicked her tongue over the head of my dick and moaned while caught up in the act. I was really young when I experienced her grown lips on me for the first time and no matter how many times women blessed me, head has never gotten old.

I sucked in my bottom lip and dropped my head back against the couch. My eyes were closed when I sensed the other one climb over the furniture and take her seat on top of me. The gelled slickness of her bare pussy lips against my abs made my dick twitch in the other one's mouth.

My eyes were still shut when she pressed her lips to my neck, shorty down below still putting in good work coaxing a groan from deep within me.

"You can't leave," the one on top of me whispered in my ear.

My eyelids weighed too much to keep open, but I lifted them long enough to lock eyes with hers. Her breasts sat high on her chest, nipples erect. I placed the blunt between my lips to free my hands. Cupped her breasts next, then positioned her nipples against the webbings of my fingers and squeezed. I groaned again, not at the weight of her breasts in my hands, at the neck game the woman below me delivered effortlessly.

The breasts were fake on the one on top of me. I measured the hardened weight of silicone gel against my fingertips. Not uncommon in this state. I didn't prefer them, but shit, for the night? They would do.

"Says it right here," she continued, her fingers outlining my left pec. I didn't have to glance down to see what she referenced.

"*Property of La La Land,*" she read. "You belong here. You're ours."

"That means a little more than you think, shorty," I voiced low.

She gently removed one of my hands off her breast and lowered it between her thighs. With her hand on top of mine, she pressed my fingers against her slick clit and I stroked it at her insistence.

"God." She tossed her head back and moaned to herself. "It should be criminal for you to be this fine, you know that right?"

I left her question unanswered. Kept my hand busy in that spot, puffed my blunt, and leaned my head against the couch as the rhythm of the one with my dick in her mouth intensified. My eyes fluttered closed as I held the picture of a face in my mind of a woman who lived nowhere near here.

Hadn't seen her in person in over ten years, but I checked in on her from time to time via social media, mostly to see the smile attached to the face and her dark gray eyes.

My high school sweetheart I swore I'd marry.

Fucked that up royally.

I moaned when short haircut on the floor took me all the way into her mouth, relaxing her throat just right and tightening the grip of her jaw around my dick. Her bobbing became more concise. The act made me plant the pads of my feet firm against the ground to brace myself to nut.

"Yeah, shorty." I stretched my hand in her direction to palm her head, guiding her moves. "Just like that."

She couldn't hear me. The volume in the music was way too high in the penthouse to hear a damn thing.

"I wanna come with you, Pryce," the girl on top of me whispered in my ear. She ground her sex against my fingers harder and I moved in accordance to her movements.

We were all audible in that room. Loud as hell, actually. The best sound on the planet was hearing a woman's moans over mine. So imagine how two sounded. Damn near celestial.

My jaw slacked in response to it all. The girl on top of me trembled.

"Fuck," I breathed through bared teeth.

The length of me spasmed and spasmed again. I lifted off the couch no more than an inch to keep myself connected to the woman on the floor below me, not wanting her to release me as I released. She obliged, relaxing her throat even more than before and allowing my seed to flow without pulling off. She swallowed all I sputtered while I pumped my waist back and forth in the air beneath her, possessed with riding my nut out until the very end.

I fell back against the couch, sated. Still rock hard, but sated.

Shorty on top of me leaned forward, close to my ear, and whispered, "I wanna do that again."

I peeked around her to find the other one reach in front of herself for the condoms sprawled on the couch cushion beside me. She ripped opened a condom and sheathed my erection before rising off her knees. That woman moved in effortless coordination, making it clear her moves were practiced. She'd done this very thing enough times with ample sense on how not to wreck the flow.

With my hand still in position against shorty on top of me, I took another puff from my blunt then slid my finger past her wet folds and into warmth. She tossed her head back and rolled her hips against my hand.

The one below me stood with her legs astride my knees and squatted into position over my erection, her back facing the two of us. As she balanced herself on the arches of her feet and slid down my rod slowly, filling herself of me, I dropped my head back against the couch, my fingers still working, my mind drifting elsewhere again.

Tonight was the usual out here. It was easy actually. Two females was a light night. I was used to more. Why the fuck not? I got it thrown at me. The way I saw it was, some people de-stressed by exercising, some even through working. I liked to fuck, that was how *I* relaxed. All I ever had to do was show up to receive the fanfare needed to satisfy me for an evening, anyway.

But honestly, like for real, for real? My life was losing horsepower. Not my body; something deep inside me had reached its point of exhaustion with how I was living. My late thirties were peeking at me from around the corner and the life I lived was aging me within.

Their moans traveled around me, swallowing the bass in the beat that dropped in the song.

I enjoyed this though, *please* know that I did. New pussy is always great pussy, especially when it doesn't have any strings attached like the two pussies I dealt with tonight. But it wasn't the best. It was what it was; random, temporary. No substance, no potential for growth past the moment. Just available for a night. Nothing to think about later. I'd probably put more thought on the gum I spit out earlier than on what was happening in that instance.

I needed more. I just wasn't sure what that *more* was. But I knew it wasn't in this room. I knew where to get it though because I had it once before.

The kind of *more* I needed in my life was something evergreen. The kind of affection that disarmed and sedated, putting me at ease. Real and trusting enough to tame me. To let my guard down and just be.

My eyes focused up at the ceiling and on the chandelier dimmed and sparkling overhead. I blew smoke that way and watched it cloud my view. The walls on the beauty riding me drew in and tightened around my dick. I groaned in response.

I let the blunt hang from my mouth as I stretched my free hand past the one on top of me to the one riding me. Smoothed my hands around the curve of her waist and slid my middle finger to her clit below the hood.

She rode harder the moment I stroked her tiny ball.

I ran my fingers over both their swollen nubs with the same cadence and speed, the two of them shaking against my frame out of sync. Their sex cries ricocheted off the penthouse's silk upholstered walls. The shit was like magic. Sex was a production to me, a performance when done the right way, and I enjoyed the show.

I drew in smoke, then let it free through my nose as I joined the chorus of moans. My rider's walls clenched, then released uncontrollably and repeatedly around the length of me. She dug her nails into my knees to brace herself.

She was coming and hard.

They both shuddered, in fact. Although the one bouncing on my dick held up good around me, *she* wasn't *her*... Leelah.

Neither one of them were her. One million of these broads couldn't amount to half the woman Leelah was to me.

The one woman who made me experience fireworks whenever I was inside of her. Turned my thoughts to drifting clouds when our bodies touched, and I took her to a place neither one of us wanted to return from.

That was over ten years ago, though. The possibility existed that the loving wasn't the same anymore, but I wanted to find that out for myself. I needed to find that out for myself.

When sweetheart riding me reached the end of her ride, she disconnected and dropped to the floor at my feet, panting for air, a satisfied smile plastered along her face.

"That monster got my legs weak," she said through her giggles. I watched her breasts rise and fall below me as she fought to pull in air.

I focused my eyes up at the one on top of me, still grounding her hips against my hand.

With my free hand, I picked up another condom with the pinch of my fingers and brought it to my mouth to tear open. She paused, rolling her hips when she noticed the gold wrapper in the grip of my teeth.

With my other hand, I pulled the used rubber off, tossed it overhead, then rolled the new one over my erection.

She glanced behind herself, then back at me with a knowing smile.

I held her at the waist and slid her down my torso, lifting her high enough to slide in between her walls. Her jaw dropped slowly, her eyes locked on mine as her walls gave way.

"Oh, damn!" she shouted.

"I want you to take it all for me," I told her, helping her to take her seat and only stopping when no more of me could fit. "Can you do that?"

"*Mm-hmm.*"

"Good girl." I slapped her ass. "Now show me."

She took her time, oscillating her hips. I lolled my head over the couch once again, closing my eyes when the rhythm she produced turned into something I could get into. Allowing her to be a substitute like the others before her.

Because tonight, I'd make it about them, but when the sun rose over these Cali hills, I was all Leelah's, if she'd have me.

THREE

LEELAH

"It's time to take back your first love," I told my client, Valerie. She lounged on the couch across from me. "Go for a run and do it solo. Get re-acclimated with your love of running."

"A *run?*" she asked, eyes wild with discernment. "I told you I don't have time to run anymore. I barely have the time to think, much less exercise like I used to, Leelah. The kids are away for camp this summer, true, but I've been doing enough *running* around getting things organized for school in the fall. That's just two months away! I can't possibly—"

"Clear your mind in a park somewhere with a run?" I interjected with a smile. "Your first week here, you revealed to me, running was an outlet you missed. Life, work, and family have taken priority, and that's understandable, but I'll never forget the light in your eyes when you spoke of your multi-mile runs. It's time we get that light back."

She inhaled a deep breath and nodded reluctantly.

"Look," I continued. "You can stay close by but I would recommend you go for a drive to a place like upstate. Maybe *Bear Mountain State Park*. It has the most stunning open spaces filled with trees, hills, and views. Perfect for a run, trek, or hike, making it an ideal setting to ground yourself in the now and give your anxious thoughts a rest."

She smiled. "You make it sound *so* easy to just—"

"Go?" I finished. "Be carefree for a day and let others worry about the mundane? Like we've agreed you need to do, and pronto?"

She bounced her head up and down.

"A good friend of mine always says things are hard when we say they're hard and they're easy when we decide they're easy because our thoughts become things."

Valerie scoffed a laugh. "So simple and very true."

"Our session goals have all been like tiny building blocks, assisting with getting you back to *you*. There's nothing wrong and everything right with doing what brings you joy too, Val. And running brought you the kind of joy you can't buy. Your words. Do you remember telling me that?"

"I honestly can't believe you remembered that."

"Go for a run, Val. It's just a run. Physical activity will do you a lot of good, especially when it was a source of happiness once before. It will also give you an opportunity to memorize the affirmations we brainstormed together in past sessions. Recite them in your time alone, surrounded by trees and abundant space. When you put yourself in larger-than-life spaces, it puts things in perspective and helps you realize how tiny your problems are compared to life's wonders." I crossed my legs and leaned forward. "You have spent so much time putting yourself last and being everything to everybody and that's fine. But at some point, you have to offer that same compassion to yourself. Your cup is close to empty and you actually feel guilty about catering to yourself. If you allow life to deplete you, you will have nothing left to give your family which will be a disservice to you and them. Pour back into yourself so that your cup can run over and they can enjoy and benefit from your presence."

"But a run?" she repeated.

"Yes, a run." I closed my black notebook and stood up. "Sounds non-transformative and a step backwards, but I'm telling you from experience a run in *Bear Mountain State Park* does wonders for the psyche. I promise, you'll feel like your old self. You'll be refreshed and your husband and kids will appreciate this treat to yourself more than you think."

Valerie grabbed her designer label tote and stood to her feet.

"And," I added, as I approached her and took her hand, "I believe my suggestion will help with reducing those anxiety attacks even more and you'll put them under control the more you give yourself grace and spend time alone to listen to your inner narrator. It isn't the end all be all. Admittedly, your anxiety attacks will require more than just one run in a park upstate, but it's a necessary small step toward healing. You have so much going on around you, that your mind becomes as chaotic as your surroundings. Serving as everything to everybody can get noisy up here." I pointed at my temples. "Mute that a little. Me time with a run far from here. I'm excited to hear how this worked out for you next week."

"I can't wait to share. I'm actually curious to see if this will even work." Valerie stepped closer for a hug. "But I'm confident it will because everything else you've suggested has. Thank you so much for all you do." She moved out of her hug and held both of my hands again.

Valerie was in her early 40s, but stress had aged her by a few more years. A cheating husband, demanding ungrateful pre-teens for kids. They were running her ragged. She wasn't the only one. This was my client demographic. Close to middle-aged women overwhelmed but with enough money to fan the tears from their eyes, just not enough to buy the happiness that bared no price tag.

"Before seeing you, I was so close to losing it."

"Well, you're doing great, Val," I told her with a smile. "So next week?"

She rubbed her hands together. "Yes, next week."

I leaned inward as she pulled me into another hug, then made her way out my office door.

Back in front of my desk, I plopped down into my leather chair.

Everything in my office was modest. I didn't have the urge to overdo it, although I often got the bug to redecorate every once in a while. In the SoHo section of the city my practice drew in the usual affluent resident, most of them Manhattanites who lived in the area. These people were used to a certain living, yet they found comfort in the basic make up of my office. A small wood table with a leather chair was my desk. On that desk were three succulent plants, an hourglass, and my computer screen. Two leather armchairs, a sofa, coffee table, and a book-case completed my quaint space. Honestly, the showstopper was the built-in wall waterfall outside in reception. It offered a soothing atmosphere for clients who had to wait to meet with me. It's the little things that make a big difference in this field.

While unbuttoning my blazer to remove and drape over my chair, my secretary, April, a young first-year graduate student in her early twenties, popped her head past the door and into my office.

"Got a minute?" she asked, "or should I come back in a few?"

I gestured with my hand for her to step in, and she took a seat in one of the plush armchairs in front of my desk.

"You received a few calls while you were with Mrs. Stevenson."

I leaned back in my chair. "Tell me about them."

"The first one was from Mrs. Tanner. She wanted me to ask if you can fit her in for tomorrow at noon."

"Check my calendar, and if I'm free, put her in. If I'm not, put her in the next available time slot."

"Done." April directed her eyes down while writing on her notepad. "Next, you received a call from a Liz Peters who asked if you two can meet at 6 p.m. instead of 7 p.m. on Thursday?"

"Call her back and tell her 6 p.m. is perfect."

April wrote a few words and pointed her beaming eyes my way. "Last," she sang, taking a breath, her big smile spreading across her face this time, "Pryce Williams's manager called."

I stopped breathing for a moment.

"Actually he called a few times." She stood up and approached my desk, ripping out a page from her notepad along the way. "He asked that you call him back as soon as possible. This is the phone number he told me to give you."

"Uh-huh?" I stared down at the paper she placed in front of me and folded my lips into my mouth.

"Pryce Williams?!" She blushed. "*You* know Pryce Williams?"

"*I wish I didn't*," was what I wanted to reply with.

"*Know* is a strong word, April." I picked up the paper, my eyes damn near boring a hole into the phone number. "Okay, thanks for the updates. You can head out to make your calls."

"Will do," she replied, prancing out my office and closing my door behind her.

The moment she left, I let out the breath I'd been holding in. I raked my fingers through my curls and dropped my head back against my leather chair.

"What the hell does he *want*?" I whined to myself.

The *he* was Pryce and not his manager Marc because if I had to bet on it, Pryce was using Marc to get to me.

The last person I needed around me or to even hear from was Pryce.

I had a sneaky suspicion he'd reach out when I heard the news at the bar about him possibly signing with the *Ballers*. I was aware he'd visit New York from time to time. According to gossip websites, he owned a loft in Tribeca, not far from me. But all the years I've lived there we'd never bumped into each other nor has he reached out to me aside from years ago when he first got drafted, thank God. New York is a huge city so not running into each other on the street wasn't uncommon. But why the hell was he reaching out *now*, albeit through his best friend?

It had been over ten years since we'd last spoken. Over a decade and still my breathing altered simply by the mention of his name. It was the complete opposite back when we were teenagers.

I was a freshman, only in *Turner High School* for two whole weeks before he took notice of me. Pryce was a welcomed distraction. My mother had passed away the summer before I started school, and my heart was still aching from her sudden absence. But the moment Pryce and my eyes met in the school's crowded hallway, I just knew deep in me I'd found my new reason to smile.

Pryce was a senior, big guy on campus type. Every girl wanted to have his arm wrapped around them, including the cheerleaders who obsessed over Pryce, but the boy had eyes for me. For what? I was still clueless about. Something drew Pryce to me and me to him, though. He asked me out and a week later we were official.

I wasn't immune to his handsome. He was heartthrob fine. In high school, Pryce appeared older than a lot of guys in school, and I think that's what appealed to me. He was tall, like extremely tall. Everyone predicted he'd play for the *NBA* before he participated in the draft. You can't be 6'11 and punching in at a place with regular ceilings.

I chuckled to myself at the thought.

From the moment we started dating, I settled into the idea of marrying him. At 14, I decided I would be his wife and the mother of his children, a lot of them, as many as he wanted. Be barefoot and pregnant in some mansion far out of New York.

My little 14-years-old self was ready for a commitment like that. I'd romanticized the idea of falling in love young after listening to an anthology worth of stories narrated by my late mother. I'd memorized my parents' love story and could recite it by heart, that's how many times she told it. She'd reminisce about how she and my father bumped into each other in the halls of their high school their first year. The gleam in her eyes and the blush in her cheeks were damn near contagious every time she detailed their love at first sight.

I wanted that, so badly, and I wanted that feeling as soon as I could get it. It was probably one of the biggest reasons high school seemed so appealing.

"Fool," I chastised myself as I pressed my hand to my forehead and scrubbed my brows.

That was one of the reasons I had sex with Pryce for the first time on my sixteenth birthday.

It was the summer before my junior year in high school and his second year in college. We'd been dating for almost three years, and he'd practiced patience in terms of being intimate. Pryce and I had done everything else besides "it." Head was something he liked a lot, and I enjoyed doing. His reactions and the total control I had over him with my mouth around the length of him was a huge turn on. Here I was, regular ass Leelah Waters making the most popular guy on his college campus vulnerable and dependent on me bringing him to that point of no return.

So when my birthday rolled around on July 1st, I told him what I wanted for my present. Ecstatic couldn't begin to describe Pryce's reaction to the news. He invested a lot of time and effort into making things as special as possible. He bought roses and scattered them all over his dorm room floor. Pryce spared no expense that night in order to make things special. He didn't share the space with anyone, it was only him, so we had the privacy.

Pryce played soft music, a Body & Soul cd. I remembered the violins in

Avant and Keke Wyatt's "My First Love" strumming as Pryce took his position over me. He balanced himself on his forearms and kissed me deep.

My heart pounded in my chest. I was sure he could not only hear it but count the beats too. My nerves were heightened not because I believed I was making a big mistake. I was concerned that things would change between us. Pryce considered me to be his precious gem, flawless in his eyes. He handled me with so much care those years we dated pre-sex. I told him I wanted to wait until marriage, and he never challenged that. Never pushed for me to change my mind.

I believed he deserved this. I believed he earned me. So I figured, I plan to marry him anyway. Might as well get this part over with.

Pryce was a big guy and all over. From his bulbous head on his shoulders to his bigger than life feet. And as for between his legs, he had more than enough to make me cringe a little as he tried to guide himself inside of me.

"You real tight, La," he groaned in my ear. "Maybe we should stop."

I shook my head and pressed my hand to his backside. "No, please don't."

"Your face is telling me something different," he whispered with a smirk.

"It hurts a little, but I promise I'm okay."

He exhaled and tried again, this time with more gusto.

A few deep thrusts, sighs of frustration, and toying with my clit later, I gasped when he worked himself in.

Pryce filled me. Breathing wasn't an option in that moment. I shut my eyes tight, releasing the tension when the warmth of his mouth covered mine.

Pryce's kisses always stopped time for me. Nothing outside of him ever mattered when our tongues tangled.

He didn't rush as promised, but I couldn't ignore the sting of us being physical until it was overshadowed by something else.

Tears welled in my eyes, clouding my vision as I grew still beneath him. My sister, Gena, tried her hardest to talk me out of doing this. When she realized I was gung-ho on going through with it, she tried her hand at eliciting fear in me by warning me not to expect much from my first time because losing my virginity would hurt like shit.

Pryce must have been aware of this because amid his strokes he positioned his hand between us to caress my clit in time with his thrusts. The pain mixed with pleasure numbed my mind. I became still beneath him when a rush of something else grabbed any breath I had left in me and held it captive.

The guttural moan that vibrated from my throat I didn't even recognize. Pryce had paid special attention to my clit several times before we had sex, but I'd felt nothing like I did the first time he circled his fingertip around the tiny ball while inside of me. The sensation made me want to stop, but also to keep going at the same time. It was confusing and glorious simultaneously. Had the same angst and allure as a thunderstorm. All I could do was moan and bare it, curious where the storm brewing inside me would lead to if I stuck this out and didn't fold from the pain.

"Shh," he whispered on my lips. His tongue slid into my mouth next, which helped to muffle my cries.

My back arched off his full-sized bed, and I turned my head away from him. I didn't want to break the kiss, but I didn't want to get distracted and have this unfamiliar stir inside me, the one that felt so good, disappear either. Needed to hang on to the pleasure and ignore the pain as long as I could to feel it to the end.

"Pryce," I whispered through breaths as pressure built within. My walls pulsed and fluttered around his girth, the flutters growing stronger with each stroke. I shut my eyes and kept inhaling, forgetting to exhale, feeling seconds away from imploding. "Something... is... happening... to me."

"Mmm-hmm," he replied, rocking into me, slowing his speed and covering my mouth with his again. "I feel it happening to you too. Just relax, okay baby? Breathe with me."

I swear I saw stars as my body vibrated without control. My eyes rolled to the back of my skull and I let them. I just gave in to everything.

"You're coming for me right now." He whispered in my mouth, holding me tight and keeping pace. "And you look so fucking beautiful doing it, La. My God."

"It feels so... good," I mewled, squeezing my eyes shut.

"It's gonna feel better," he promised. "Just go with it, aight? I got you."

The blare of my ringer pulled me out of my thoughts.

I shook my head to gain some control over myself. My hand was reaching for my bag, then my phone, my fingers clicking the answer button before I could even process the action.

"This is Leelah."

"Dr. Waters, actually," the voice said on the other end. I recognized it instantly.

A smile tugged at my lips as I leaned back in my seat. "You're damn right."

Marc chuckled on the other end of my phone and I joined in. "What's good, Leelah?"

"Life. But I'm sure not as good as yours."

Marc Maldonado. Pryce's best friend. This guy was like Pryce's family. If you saw Pryce, you'd see Marc. They were like brothers, and these days Marc was Pryce's manager.

"Ahh, well you know." He chuckled. "I can't complain. How you been, sis?"

"Maintaining," I replied.

"That sexy phone voice definitely has been maintained."

I kissed my teeth. "Still a corny ass flirter, I see."

He snorted a laugh.

"So what's up?" I crossed my legs. "It's clear to me you didn't dial my number to only say, *hey*, or hear my sexy voice."

"Of course I did. Why would you say that?"

"Because you've been blowing up my business line all day according to my secretary. Like some kind of campaign manager days before an election. And now I'm curious about how you got my mobile number."

"I have my ways of acquiring info."

"Oh, I bet, Marc."

He chuckled. "So... Your secretary's been giving you my messages?"

"She has." I focused on the raw brick wall in my office. "I was in with a client when you called."

"And now?"

"I'm free."

"Free enough to meet with Pryce?"

I straightened my back in my chair. Words couldn't leave my lips.

My mouth was open, the thoughts were there, but I couldn't say anything.

"Leelah?" Marc called. "Please tell me you're still there."

Another moment of silence.

"Leelah?"

Finally, I asked, "Meet with Pryce *for what*?"

He exhaled into the phone. "He needs to see you."

My eyes moved around my office. "He needs to see me? For what, exactly?"

"Uh..." Marc stammered. "He, uh... got one of those things... an um... a... *whatchamacall* those things?" I picked up on him snapping his fingers on the other end of the line the way he did when he tried to recall the forgotten. Finally he blurted, "An addiction."

I grimaced. "An addiction?"

"Yeah. A um..." He paused for a moment longer as if he were thinking some more. "A sex addiction." He snapped his fingers once again. "Yes, that's it. Pryce has a sex addiction."

The laugh that bellowed from my gut shocked me. It would have been insensitive with anyone else and I never would have done that with a client but this was Marc and we were talking about Pryce having a sex addiction which was absolute...

"Bullshit," I told him.

"Nah, for real," Marc defended. "Like, it's bad La. Make time to sit with him."

"Did he shower this morning?"

"Wh-what? Did he shower this morning?"

"Yes. *Did* Pryce shower this morning? Eat anything?"

"Why are you asking me that?! I don't know if the man showered. I think so."

"Have you seen him today?"

He exhaled into the phone. "Of course I've *seen* him, La. I see Pryce almost every day."

"Okay, then yes, you would know if he showered. If he hadn't, you would smell he hadn't and since you didn't notice a ripe odor on him, that means he did shower which also means he's good." I crossed my legs in my seat. "Sex addiction affects a person's quality of life."

"Leelah."

"All they can think about is sex and satisfying the reward center in their brain that sex often stimulates. If he's eaten and washed his ass, a sex addiction is not it."

So fine; I was exaggerating a bit, maybe a lot, but I had to call Marc's bluff. It was either that or agree to see Pryce, and *that* was *not* happening.

"Pryce just likes sex," I continued, "probably a little too much these days, but he doesn't need help with that, okay? He needs discipline."

"Leelah, *please*," Marc grumbled next. "I am *begging* you to see him. Sit down with him for an, uh, evaluation, or whatever you therapists do and see for yourself."

I scoffed at his gall. Marc has never, ever, been short of gall.

"Just meet with him once."

"Marc—"

"For me," he interjected. "Do this for me, La, please."

I rolled my eyes closed and dropped my head back against my chair. "I'll tell you what... I'll think about it."

"La," he whined.

"It's not a no," I explained. "I need to check my schedule."

And my mental stability.

"Once I do that," I continued, "and everything seems clear, I *may* be able to pencil him in."

"How soon can you confirm?"

"By the end of the week."

"I need a day, La," he pushed.

I rolled my eyes closed again. "Then Friday."

A perfect day to tell you no because I will definitely be telling you no.

"Aight, I'll take that!"

I sighed in defeat.

"I've told you over a million times that you've always been my favorite, La," Marc reminded. "And I've never lied when I said that. Not one single time."

I tried to wrestle the smile off my lips, but the damn thing won.

"In my eyes you'll *always* be Mrs. Williams."

That was the nickname Marc gave me when Pryce and I were

together. One of the biggest supporters of me and Pryce. I wonder where he was when Pryce was out there ruining our relationship.

"If that was it, I have to go, Marc."

"Yeah, of course," he replied. "I'll wait for your phone call. It was great hearing your voice again, La."

"Likewise."

"We'll talk soon."

With that, I ended the call and dropped my device on my desk.

"Sex addiction," I remarked, twisting my lips to one side while biting inside my bottom lip. "What are they up to?"

Four

"Yo, what's good, Pryce?" Jaleel asked on the other end of my phone.

"Ain't nothin' much." I moved around my room, picking up clothes and tossing them into my wicker hamper. "Just chillin at the moment. What's good with you?"

I'd returned home for the summer, arriving the night before. Home would have been in the borough of Brooklyn, but my loft was in the city, Tribeca to be exact.

"Everything, especially after hearing you're back for the whole summer," he said. "We should link up while you out here. Let me give you the *Bronx Ballers* welcome."

"The team owner and your coach must've put you up to that."

I'd been in talks with my agent, who still resided in Cali, regarding my plans. But the talk with my boy Marc, who was also my manager, was most important. Of course, discussions revolving around business took center stage between us. There were a few interviews I needed to sit for while in New York. But honestly? What I cared about most was getting in contact with Leelah.

I planned to call her the moment I stepped off the plane the night before, but Marc insisted I hold off on it. For what, I wasn't sure.

I mean, I knew *why*. For sure, shorty had no interest in hearing from me, ever. But I had to shoot my shot, you know? Turn the knob to see for myself if that door was really closed. And even if it were, I had no plans of giving up without really giving it my all to earn her back.

"Coach and I may have had a little discussion." Jaleel snickered. "But he didn't have to convince me to reach out. You know you my boy. So what's up?"

Jaleel Gordon played the shooting guard position for the *Bronx Ballers* and was a good friend of mine in the league. We balled a few games together, my team the *Oakland Flames* besting his team most of the time, but it has always been love between us. Plus, Jaleel always played solid games. It was his team that sucked.

"No doubt, we can definitely chill," I replied. "You stay out in Rochester, right?"

"Nah." His voice took on a heavier tone. "Uh, I'm... I'm staying out here in the city right now. Eva and I are separated. She's talking about divorce all up in my ear."

"Damn, really?" I paused in my steps toward my door. "I'm sorry to hear that."

"Not as sorry as I am. I'm hoping it's temporary, but you know how that go. Just tryna give E her space or whatever."

"Hmph."

"Anyway, hit me up when you're free next and let's make this happen."

"No doubt." I pulled open my bedroom door. "I'll hit you back tonight."

After finishing up the call with Jaleel, I stepped down my stairs, headed to the kitchen. I saw Marc sitting at the island bar typing away on his phone.

Marc has been my boy since high school. He and I ran through the halls and ducked below short doorways to enter classrooms back in the day. My boy used to hype me up during my games, practice with me on the basketball court in the neighborhood park. We'd shoot jump shots through net-less rims and execute layups on hoops with missing back-boards. So, at 20-years-old, before the ink could dry on my newly signed contract to play for the *Oakland Flames*, it was a no-brainer that my boy would come out there with me.

"What's good, what's good?" I greeted when I reached the bottom step.

"This interview you got with *For The Culture* in two weeks." He replied. "They just emailed me the questions, most of which are about your final decision."

I chuckled.

"Everybody out here speculating. Will he, won't he?"

"Hmph." I padded toward my Subzero fridge to grab a bottle of water.

Marc followed me with his slanted eyes. "You got niggas out here taking bets on you heading back to Oakland once you come to your senses."

"Oh word?"

"Word."

"Well, shit, place your bet too, Marc," I insisted. "Bet I'll play for the *Ballers*."

He twisted his lips to one side as if to challenge me.

"Yo, dead ass." I took a seat opposite him. "You'll make mad bank."

"So you're considering staying out *here* for real?"

I shrugged. "That depends. Got in touch with Leelah?"

His eyes closed, and he leaned back in his seat.

"That bad, huh?"

"She said she'll think about it."

I shut my eyes and hung my head forward.

"And that's after I told her some shit."

I lifted my gaze to him. "*Some shit* like what?"

He clapped his hands once. "So check it - I may have told her you have a little, ity bity, *tiny*... sex addiction."

My eyes widened. "Marc?"

"Look, she refused to hear anything else."

"A sex addiction though?!" I hollered. "Out of all the fucking things, man?"

"Calm down." Marc raised his hands, palms facing me. "It was the first thing that came to mind. If I didn't say that, it would have been a hard no from her for sure. Trust me, bruh. She was not having it."

I grunted, then hung my head back between my shoulders this time. "Aight, aight, so what? You followed up with her?"

"I just spoke with her yesterday."

I leveled my head and my gaze then told him, "Follow up with her today."

"That's not how this will work."

I kissed my teeth.

"She needs some time to process." He ran his hand down his face. "She knows you're here. That's a start."

"I don't got *time*, Marc. I gotta make this decision before October, well before October. I'm expected to report for a physical—"

"Decision? Wait, hold up. Hold. *Up.*" He scooted forward in his seat. "*You* playing for the *Ballers* depends on if La gives you another shot?"

"Honestly?" I dragged my hands down the length of my beard. "Yeah."

"The fuck?!" Marc stared at me. "So if she says yes—"

"Then I'm staying."

"You sure? Pryce, you're willing to risk your whole career and everything? You got endorsements riding on you staying in Oakland. Are you ready to make that move with her like *that*?"

I pushed my tongue against my cheek. "I think so."

"You *think* so? Yo, you got businesses out there," he added. "The sneaker store, your rental properties—"

"I got the indoor basketball gyms out here in New York, though. I can always travel for the other stuff."

"Pryce, bruh, the *Ballers* are trash, my dude. Trash!" He scratched his nose, a nervous habit. "Just saying that team's name is making me itch. Do you realize what the fuck you're saying to me right now?"

"Man, look, I'm ready, aight?" I tapped the bar island with a closed fist for emphasis. "I'm willing to dead all that Cali shit, and plant my ass right here in this state and with the *Ballers* for her."

"Says the nigga who brought two fucking women to his penthouse to blow their backs out for hours on end just two nights ago. And on a Sunday at that. The day set aside for the lord."

"That was farewell pussy. That shit didn't count."

Marc waved his hand at me. "It's always farewell pussy to you. Your thinking is what got you in this mess with Leelah to begin with."

There was no denying that. Marc spoke facts.

"This was the last game of the season," Courtney reminded. "We should celebrate. Let me congratulate you the right way."

Courtney Simmons was a cute sophomore with thick pink lips who cheered for the LU Blackbirds. I was a month away from completing my second year at Langston University and on a natural high after shooting the winning shot with only two seconds on the clock. The team damn near carried me off the courts on their shoulders, that's how excited we were. March Madness had brought some much needed attention to the university and winning the final game was major.

There were whispers a few sports agents watched from the skybox at The Garden and couldn't take their eyes off me. They promised me inclusion in the draft once I declared my eligibility, and that left me hype too.

What I really wanted to do was call up my girl, Leelah. She acted like a cheerleader for me from her seat but had to return home with her dad and sister since the game finished late and we left MSG way past curfew to chill on campus. Guests weren't allowed in the dorms after a certain hour, and the hour for visits had passed long ago.

So there I was with Courtney. Compared to Leelah, Court's body wasn't much to brag about, but Courtney knew how to flirt and understood all the right things to say which she unleashed on me that night.

I wasn't thinking when her hand found a home on my crotch.

"You know I got a girl, right?"

"Yeah, a girl." She licked her lips. "You need a woman."

I dropped my head forward to scratch the back of my head.

"But if you want to keep it hush." She ran her hand up to my chest. "I won't tell."

We stared into each other's eyes. I knew better. Leelah had my heart. Before her, I foolishly believed I fell in love with my neighbor, Renee. Renee was an older woman and the person who taught me everything I knew about women. But when Leelah stepped through the halls on the first day of school, my last year at Turner High, she captured everything in me. My attention, my mind, and most importantly, my heart.

So, what the fuck was I doing?

The want to ask Courtney to leave my room was there. My words with her instructions to exit sat right at the tip of my tongue, but so did my curiosity. I'd been teaching Leelah what to do in bed. Giving head, she needed no directions, but everything else felt like a lesson plan, although I enjoyed doing even that with her. Still, sometimes it didn't feel like enough. I was young, not fully aware of the violation I was committing on a girl as dope as Leelah. Consequences be damned, I chose to be selfish over being loyal. In the moment, the decision didn't seem like a big deal. I had no idea how I was altering my future by entertaining that girl Courtney.

Courtney pulled her shirt up and over her head, then dropped her varsity shorts, and I quickly shed my morals along with the rest of her clothes.

Shorty stood before me wearing nothing. Light brown nipples erect, pussy so wet it made the fine hairs around the lips glisten.

I licked my lips and grabbed her by the hips and it was over. Everything was over 24-hours after that, and the decision to wreck everything wasn't even worth it.

"Yo Pryce!" Marc clapped his hands in my face. "Wake the fuck up."

I shook my head in an effort to ground myself back in the now.

"Always daydreaming." He chuckled while shaking his head. "It's a wonder you won yet another Defensive player of the year trophy as much as your ass be spacing out."

"I don't space out on the court." I unscrewed the top off the bottle and took a swig. "This mind of mine is sharp as a tact out there."

"*Mmm-hmm.*"

"Make this shit happen for me, Marc."

We held our stares across from one another.

I added, "I *need* to see her."

He ran his hand across the back of his neck and grunted.

Marc and Leelah had history. His mother and her mother were good friends. She and Marc spent a lot of time together the summer before Leelah's freshman year and after her mother passed away only a few days after Leelah's fourteenth birthday. Marc introduced me to Leelah when I told him about seeing her in the halls that first week of school. Without hesitation, Marc hooked us up. And with that same lack of hesitation, cursed my ass out and even squared up when I broke her heart.

"I need to see her like I need air, my dude."

"Aight, man. I'mma do my very best to make it happen for you. That's my word."

Marc held his hand out, and we dapped before bumping fists.

"Cool." I puffed out my chest, satisfied with him giving me his word. "I appreciate you."

FIVE

LEELAH

"You look great," my therapist, Liz, complimented.

"If only I could feel how I look." I smiled as I took a seat at the edge of the chaise across from her desk. "You redecorated again."

She beamed. "Added a few more African pieces I picked up during my travels. My interior decorator, Nubia... I told you about her, right?

"Yes, Nubia Merci."

"Right! Well, she added a few more crystals, another floor plant, and voila!"

"I like it." I glanced around me. "My office vibe is minimalist, but I can get into this."

A therapist seeing a therapist. It's very common. Therapists needed someone to offload on, too. The stories we hear from clients, the stress of being an ear to others, can be overbearing. So I came here for the stability, and for other reasons. For me, I needed to talk to Liz to preserve my sanity. Though our relationship has morphed into a friendship, I'd been seeing her for the past two years, seeking her guidance with my life.

It seems I have a gift for solving everyone else's problems except my own.

"Thank you for coming in earlier than usual," she said.

"Oh, that's no problem." I sighed. "I was eager for my session today, anyway. Trust me."

"Long day?" she asked, pulling out her black notebook and placing the book on her desk.

I held up a hand. "Let's not take notes this evening, if that's okay?"

She analyzed me from her seat.

"I just..." I pinched the innermost corners of my eyes. "Let's switch off therapist a little and turn up friend. I just need a listening ear. I don't want you to follow up on the things we talk about this evening."

Liz pressed her shoulders to her leather chair. "That bad?"

I shut my eyes and exhaled through my mouth.

Liz stood from her desk to head my way.

She'd taken a seat in the armchair across from me when she asked, "Is it a patient?"

"A *potential* patient."

She bowed her head briefly, nonverbally encouraging me to continue.

My eyes moved around her office, landing on plants that decorated the floors or adorned shelves. Liz's basement office was enviable. So professional with a touch of home and a lot of class.

"My ex," I continued. "His best friend, who is also *my* friend, called me asking for my help."

Liz crossed her legs while leaning in. "The first love *ex*?"

"The only *ex* I've ever had." I covered my eyes with my hands. "And I don't know what to do."

"Well," she began, "what does he need assistance with?"

"Apparently a sex addiction."

Her mouth formed an *O*.

"But the claim is bullshit," I insisted. "I don't need a psychic to tell me he's bullshitting me. And I can't help the guilt that builds in me for saying that out loud because his addiction could very well be true, but I don't trust Pryce. Not after everything. So I have to believe he would lie about some shit like this."

"So what's your conundrum?"

I swallowed hard and dropped my eyes to my hands. Strumming the pad of my thumb over the gloss of my pink manicured nails, I replied, "I realized recently that I'm not over him. In fact, I *might* still be in love with him."

"Oh-kay." She folded her arms. "And here we go."

"Oh boy..."

"Leelah, it's been—"

"Over ten years." I confirmed. "Trust, I know."

"And he's the reason—"

"I binge fucked any guy who held a stare with me for more than a second. Did that throughout college and most of my twenties?" I bit at my bottom lip, nervous. "Yup, I'm aware of that too."

Liz pointed at me while balling her lips. "I would not say that. And you know I would *not* say *that*. You also understand my psychology on our responses to unfortunate situations and why we cannot blame others for our actions."

I sighed, forcing my eyes ahead to keep from rolling. "I know."

"We've covered in countless sessions, taking accountability even when influenced. Because at the end of the day—"

"We only do what we want to even when it doesn't seem that way when we do it. Liz." I smirked, holding my hands up in supplication. "You're preaching to the choir. I had a slip."

"Welcome back then." She smiled. "Do you see why I wish all my clients were therapists too?"

We both shared a laugh.

"Well, I think you should meet with him."

I locked eyes with her.

"Before the session. Sit with him outside of your office and feel him out. Feel the situation out. If you suspect the sex addiction is a hoax, you'll be able to tell this after meeting with him. You feed two birds with one seed. You meet with him to determine what he wants and you determine if he really needs your help."

I bobbed my head up and down slowly, agreeing.

"Maybe," she said leaning forward, "you can finally clue him in on your feelings."

"Which ones?" I quizzed. "That I hate him for cheating on me all those years ago or that I have never stopped loving him despite him breaking my heart?"

She shrugged. "Both?"

I scoffed while pressing my back to the back of my seat.

As hard as I tried, I couldn't quit replaying in my head the night Pryce revealed to me he'd slept with someone else. What made things worse is I had already been warned his betrayal would happen.

I was in the last few weeks of my junior year in high school when Pryce called asking if he could stop by and see me.

He'd just played a winning game a couple of days ago which my father, my sister Gena, and I were in attendance for.

I was so proud of him. My heart could burst watching him play on the courts at Madison Square Garden. He moved like a professional on those hard maple floors, blocking shots and rebounding them, even taking a few himself. He was a Center, but Pryce could do it all.

"La," he whispered in the phone. "Baby, come outside."

The hour had to be after ten. My father was away for a few days transporting goods five states away on his truck. Making a living as a trucker took up a lot of my dad's time. He spent most of his days on the road leaving me at our house with Gena, who still lived home while finishing up her doctorate in computer science instead of moving into her own place like the rest of her friends.

"Is everything okay?" I asked, sitting up in bed.

Pryce exhaled into the phone. "I'm outside in the car in front of your house."

With that, he hung up. My heart sank. The first thing I thought was he was here to breakup with me. I was expecting it, especially after my run-in with some girl who lived on his floor in the dorms.

Her name was Courtney. She was cute, tall, with really straight silky brown hair. Pryce introduced us the first week of his freshman year. He never hesitated to introduce me as his girlfriend to the people he befriended on campus. And everyone was always very welcoming, all except Courtney.

No, instead she told me one night as I left his room, "He'll be mine by the end of next year's school year."

She told me that only a few days after Pryce completed his freshman year at Langston U and moved his stuff out of his dorm room for the summer.

That fall, when he returned for his second year, her words haunted me every time Pryce and I ended a date and he had to return on campus. Things were worse when he hung up with me to go to sleep in his room to wake up for practice or classes the next day.

Attending high school and dating a college guy seemed cute to my friends, but being in a relationship with Pryce was the most stressful thing. Courtney saying that to me foolishly influenced my decision to have sex with Pryce that summer on my birthday. I didn't want for him to want anything I couldn't give him.

Marriage was my goal with him. And I wanted to wait, but I believed he and I would be husband and wife, so why delay the inevitable?

The moment I took a seat in his car and closed the door, I recognized the wrinkled look of guilt on his face, evident in his brows, that told me everything before he could. But still, I convinced myself he would never. He loved me too much to ever.

His eyes were red like he'd been crying. Pryce had this smooth milk chocolate-like skin that glowed on any other day, but that night his skin was damn near pale.

I ran my hand down his cold cheek, and he closed his eyes and leaned into my palm.

"What's the matter, baby?"

I watched his Adam's apple bobble in his throat as he swallowed hard.

Leaning forward in the passenger seat, I locked eyes with him. My chest heaved as my heart beat at a quickened pace. "Pryce, what did you do?"

"Me and this girl Courtney..."

That's all it took for the tears to fall. Between my cries, I heard him confess to having sex with her. That she took off all her clothes and approached him. How he gave in and was sorry about cheating. Pryce peppered me with so many apologies in his car, I was convinced they soiled me. I wanted to drop myself in a vat of acid to get them all off me.

"That bitch warned me," I told him. "She warned me and I didn't listen. She told me you'd be hers and she was right."

He shook his head while reaching for my hand. "She don't got me. I'm yours."

"No you're not." I threw my hands up between us. "Hell fucking no! You're not mine. Not anymore, Pryce, because the second you laid with her ass you became hers," I cried. "How could you do that to me, to us?"

"Leelah, please."

"Leelah, please?" I challenged through my teeth. "Please, what?!"

Pryce sat beside me, chest visibly rising and falling, face wet with tears, and eyes pleading for an outcome I wasn't going to allow.

"It's over," I whispered, eyes large with disbelief. Even I couldn't believe what I was saying. "It's all over."

That was literally the last time I saw him in person, and I've been trying to get my heart back from him ever since.

"So," Liz began, pulling me back in the present with her. "What do you say?"

"About?"

"Meeting up with him again, finally," she replied. "Telling him all the things you've kept on your heart all these years. I think this is an excellent opportunity for you to move past this. And if there is something there for you two..."

"Doubt that." I shook my head. "Forgiveness is a hard act for me, you're fully aware of *my* fact."

She dipped her head in agreement.

"I'll definitely think about it though, especially if it'll finally free me of him. Because that's one block I *want* removed."

"And that's good enough for me. *I'll think about it* is better than a no."

I pointed at her. "That's what I usually say."

"Whatever you do though, Leelah," she added. "Be open to the opposite of what you say you want. You know, this whole being free of him notion?"

I stared ahead at her.

"Because sometimes... not getting what we want can be a good thing."

SIX

I tried to ignore the small crowd gathering on the other side of my window as I lunched across from Marc. We dined at a corner table in *Blyss*, a restaurant bar and lounge in Manhattan known for their rooftop view.

Marc insisted we sit on the roof where they had open seating, but I didn't want a bunch of people surrounding me and asking to have their pictures taken with me.

So much for that.

Not only was my picture being taken, but a small group of people were gathering outside with me as their focus.

Paparazzi, about five of them, parked themselves on the other side of the restaurant's window, zooming in with their camera lenses from afar and snapping pictures. My security guards, three big dudes trained to kill, stood outside too but at the curb to keep everybody at a distance.

"Told your ass let's sit on the roof," Marc taunted, forking a spool of pasta pomodoro into his mouth. "Now say cheese, nigga."

"Man, fuck you." I laughed into my napkin while patting my lips clean.

I twisted my head to focus out the window and raised a hand and waved at the onlookers. A majority of the bystanders out there were women. They smiled and waved back.

"How many of them broads you think understand basketball?" Marc asked.

"These particular women? Not a one."

We both laughed.

"Speaking of women..." I scooted my chair closer.

Marc dropped his fork onto the plate and leaned back against his chair. "Pryce."

"Tell me you've gotten in touch with Leelah, man."

"I'm working on it."

I grunted. "Why is this taking *so* long, Marc?"

"My man," he replied with a jab to the table with the tip of his index finger. "We just talked about this on Tuesday. You just got here on Monday. Patience is needed for sensitive shit like this."

I sucked my teeth loud.

"Shorty is *not* happy with you at this point and time," he continued. "You said it yourself. You've tried reaching out to her in the past."

"That was years ago and right after I got drafted."

"Okay." He bobbled his head up and down. "And she didn't want to talk to you then."

"Things might be different now. It's been over ten years."

He remained quiet for a moment, staring at me. "How do you know she doesn't have a man?"

I scoffed. "Yo, fuck her man if she got one."

Marc ran his hand down his face. "This guy."

"I'm not even considering that because I don't give a shit. He's a non-factor if you ask me." I balled my lips and let the thought sit with me. Honestly, I hadn't even considered that... Leelah being with some-one. It would make sense. It's been years since we last spoke. She's a beautiful woman, a great woman. Any man would know he'd be lucky to have her. It surprised me to learn she hadn't had children yet. Knew this because I followed her under a dummy account via her social media accounts.

Stalker shit, yes, but Leelah still had my heart in her possession and I needed to let her know that in case she forgot.

"Just give me more time, P, please." He pressed his hands together like he was about to say a prayer. "Don't fuck this up for yourself."

"I got the address to her practice," I blurted.

"And what the fuck does that mean?"

I shrugged.

"Aye." Marc inhaled sharply, then pointed in my direction. "Please don't do something stupid right now."

I palmed my glass of water and brought it to my lips to sip nonchalantly. "What? Stopping by her office right now would be stupid?"

"Very." Marc bared his teeth. "It would be *very* stupid and the fact you just fucking said it is proof enough you already made your decision."

"I'm just gon' swing by and say, hey."

"Hey?!" he hollered. Marc peeked around himself and raised a hand apologetically when he noticed he'd drawn even more attention to us. His hands were over his low-cut Caesar when he said, "I swear you don't pay me enough for this shit."

I flopped back in my seat and combed my fingers through my beard. The way I would have liked things to play out was when I arrived in New York City, Leelah would have been in my arms before nightfall. I needed to see her, lay eyes on her and her on me. My decision on if I was staying or leaving Oakland depended on it.

"Please don't do this shit today," Marc pleaded across from me. "Shorty said she would get back to me by the end of the week. It's the end of the week and it's still early."

"It's 2 p.m. Marc," I replied. "End of day is approaching. Where the phone call at?"

"We still got time Pryce."

I moved my eyes away and chewed inside my lip.

What's the worst that could happen if I showed up at her office, anyway? She promised to advise Marc regarding if she could meet with me by the end of the week. I'd be saving her a phone call, if anything.

"Fuck it." I finished my water and pushed my chair back to stand up.

"Whoa, whoa!" Marc pushed his chair back too and jumped to his feet. "What the hell are you doing?"

"Look, time is of the essence," I told him. "I don't got the time to wait around. You're familiar with my style. I need to see her and I need to see her now."

"Man, you being mad spoiled, B." he mewled under his breath. Marc twisted his head from left to right, making sure we didn't have too many eyes on us. "You don't go break a woman's heart and decide when you'll reappear in her life. That's hella selfish and disrespectfully audacious. You're not even positive if you're ready to be faithful."

"What the fuck that's supposed to mean?"

He sighed. "Are you prepared to fuck only one pussy for the rest of your life?"

I stared at him.

"Because you know that's what she's in search of, right? That's what Leelah has *always* wanted. Commitment *and* loyalty to her and *only* her."

Marc lifted his hands to my shoulders and added, "You're my boy, my brother. I love you to the moon and back, but she's like my sister, too."

"For sure," I replied. "I get that."

"So then *you get* that *I have* to protect her."

"From what?"

"Pryce, from *you*."

I kissed my teeth. "Get the fuck out of here with this shit, Marc."

"I'm serious," he insisted. "You say you're ready but the other night you were with two random ass women. Three nights before that, you were at one of those orgy parties in downtown L.A. A month before that—"

"Aight, aight." I pushed his hands off me. "You made your point."

We stood there for a moment, him staring at me and my mind racing with thoughts. The one thought that wouldn't go away was seeing Leelah. I wondered if I could go another week waiting if she didn't give Marc a call by the end of the day like she promised.

"Nah," I said to myself, dipping my hand in my pocket and pulling out a wad of cash, singling out a one hundred-dollar bill, and dropping the C-note on the table. "I'm going to her office."

His eyes ballooned. "Pryce, nah, man. No!"

I turned on the heels of my *Jordans* and headed for the door.

"Fuck my life!" he whispered loud behind me. "Shit. Fine, I guess I'm going with you."

SEVEN

LEELAH

"April," I called from my desk. "Can you please get me Georgina Wallace's file from the cabinet?"

Two hours before I closed the office for the weekend, I spent the time reviewing the files of my clients to organize my questions for the upcoming week. I loved following up with them to make sure they were on track with their session goals.

"April?" I called again. "Are you hearing me?"

I rolled my head around my neck twice and rolled my shoulders once. Sitting at a desk for most of the day could be taxing on my back. I tried going to the gym and signing up for a yoga class during my lunch breaks, but I hated them both. Yoga was way too quiet and the gym too loud. I needed a comfortable middle but still hadn't found it.

"What is this girl doing right now?" I asked out loud, pushing my chair back.

Smoothing down the slight wrinkles in my blue high waist pencil pants, I balanced myself on my nude heels to head toward my office door.

"April, girl." I stepped out of my office and turned the corner to the front area. "Did you not hear me calling—"

I froze in place. Literally, I could not take another step. My muscles locked in position, but not my heart. That organ pounded, no, hammered. My jaw did no better, hanging open, my eyes growing wider, brows slowly wrinkling over them with each breath.

"La," he whispered feet away.

"Pryce?" I whispered back.

My eyes switched over to two tall black men dressed in street clothes who were as tall and wide as my office doorway. Marc was my final focal point. He stood only a few feet behind Pryce and near the two men. Marc's hands were up, palms facing me, when he mouthed, *I'm so sorry.*

"Pr... Pry." April stuttered a few inches away from me behind her desk. Her eyes were wide, and she held her hand up, jabbing her finger in the air, pointing at Pryce. "Pr... Pry..."

"Pryce Williams is here to see me?" I finished.

"Uh-huh, uh-huh," she replied, nodding her head incessantly, her eyes still glued on him.

"Thank you so much for telling me," I snarled, staring at her. "*Ahead* of time."

She whipped her head in my direction. "I am so sorry." April turned to glance at him again, her short black bob feathering the air. "He and his crew paraded in here a minute ago and I completely forgot how to use my mouth or how to do my job."

Pryce snorted a laugh.

"Oh my God," April exclaimed next, pressing a hand to her cheek. "*You're* Pryce Williams!"

"Yup," he replied, his eyes moving off hers and onto me. "That's what they tell me."

"My father is going to lose his mind when I tell him I met you! He's *such* a huge fan."

"April," I said.

"Oh my God, you are *so* fine in person."

I furrowed my brows. "April?"

"I mean, you're beautiful on TV and in magazines and stuff. But in my face? *Gahdamn!*"

"A-pril!"

"Oh, Jesus!" She covered her face with her hands. "I am so sorry, boss lady! Please forgive me, but do you see this right now? Pryce Williams is standing right *here* in the flesh!"

I blinked over to him and almost melted myself.

Not a thing had changed on him besides his facial hair that was full and highlighted the landscape around his full lips. Still the statuesque figure with arresting brown eyes. Pryce always had hair dusting his face, but these days he'd grown out a beard and the thing sent his sex appeal through the roof.

The man buzzed sex feet away from me. Him watching me like a hawk was breaking dams between my legs.

"You are *so* tall, wow!" April continued in awe. "And so fine. Oh my God, you are *so* fine."

"Okay." I raised a finger in her direction. "Enough."

She tucked her lips into her mouth and raised an apologetic hand.

My attention switched to Marc, who looked like he wanted the power to disappear into thin air.

I pointed at Pryce while still staring at Marc and asked, "What is Pryce doing here?"

Marc fixed his lips to respond when Pryce interjected with, "La."

My eyes darted over to his.

"It's *Dr.* Waters," I corrected.

A smirk pulled at his lips before he licked his lips menacingly slow. His eyes traveled south of my eyes, coasting over my breasts, waist, and hips.

"My bad," he uttered low, his eyes still outlining my curves. "*Dr.* Waters."

The way he spoke my name stole my breath right out of me. Pryce was feeling me up with his unwavering eyes, visually undressing me in a room full of people. I couldn't stop my nipples from straining against my lace bra if I tried.

"I need to talk to you," Pryce voiced, finally making eye contact again. "It's of the utmost importance that we speak privately."

I wasn't sure how long we stood there apart, but I became lost on him. Pryce was always the handsome type. Smooth, too. Always knowing the right things to say in the moment.

We must have been standing there too long because Marc cleared his throat and gestured at April, then the two men with his eyes, reminding me that we were in mixed company and I was still at work.

"Follow me," I told Pryce. "April, please get Marc and company whatever they want."

"Oh! Yes, absolutely!" April jumped up out her seat. She asked, "What can I get for everyone? Coffee, water?"

I'd already wrapped around the corner headed to my office with Pryce on my heels and didn't catch their responses.

Only a few feet away from my office door, I peeked over my shoulder to find Pryce close behind me, his eyes glued to my ass.

"Eyes focused forward."

"Easier said than done."

I shut my eyes and swallowed as much courage as I could get inside me in that short time.

I stepped into my office first and held the door open for Pryce to swagger in after me. When he passed me, his cologne grabbed me by the pussy and made it throb.

I inhaled a calming breath and closed the door. As I made my way to my desk and took a seat to create some space between us, Pryce remained standing, his eyes moving all around my office.

"Nice," he said. He buried his hands in his pockets. The man dressed himself in a simple black tee, sweats, and *Jordans*, but looked so fucking appetizing.

How annoying!

"Pryce what are you doing here?" I asked, scrubbing my brows with my fingertips.

He turned to face me.

His eyes moved all over me with a confidence he'd refined over the years. He stared at me for a moment longer and when he finally said something, it was, "Damn."

I dropped my head to mask my smile.

I'd created dozens of scenarios in my head of what I'd do and how I'd feel if I ever saw Pryce again in person. Butterflies fluttering in my belly and a smile I couldn't hold back wasn't a part of those scenarios I'd thought up. Yet, here we were.

"How is it possible?"

I ran my fingers through my bra-strap-length curls. "What?"

"That you've gotten even more stunning since we last saw each other."

Couldn't hide my smile at that point. I rolled my eyes at myself.

"Your 30s have been real good to you."

"Pryce," I purred, then cleared my throat to get that emotion out of it. "Again, *why* are you here?"

"I needed to see you."

"For?"

He moved in close to me and I pushed my chair back and away from my desk.

Pryce said nothing as he stood over me. I fought with myself not to give in to the urge to pull him into a kiss. To wrap my arms around the back of his neck and throw my tongue into his mouth to see if his kiss could still halt time for me.

But then I remembered Marc's claim.

"Is this about your addiction?" I quizzed.

He squeezed his eyes shut and stepped back, running his hand down his mouth. "Right." He scoffed. "My *addiction*."

"Pryce, let's cut the bullshit here; you do not have an addiction. Most definitely not an addiction to sex."

He challenged but lost to holding back his smirk. "If that's what Marc told you I got, that's what I got."

"You don't appear to be someone who has a sex addiction." My eyes lowered to his crotch without thought. "Seems like life is treating you fine."

"Could treat me better."

I lifted my eyes to his.

"And the only person who can heal me is you."

"Is that right?"

"It's so right."

We stared at one another for a moment longer before a huge smile spread across his lips and I bit my tongue to keep from smiling back.

"Damn, La." He brought his prayer hands to his lips and smiled even wider. "Like, *damn*, baby."

"Dr. Waters," I corrected again.

"I know that's right." He bit his bottom lip. "Keep correcting me just like that."

His lids were heavy, his signature stare of seduction. I knew it well. It was like a scorpion's stinger, paralyzing me when he flashed it my way back in the day. I was disappointed to learn it hadn't lost its potency.

"'Cause she's a doctor with her own practice doing her own thing." He sipped in air through his teeth. *Mmm, mmm, mmm.* Go 'head and flex on me then. I love to see it, beautiful."

My cheeks warmed from blushing, and I turned away to hide that. "I *hate* that you're making me blush."

"Well, I'm loving the view."

Laugh lines framed my lips as a smile pulled my mouth up, revealing all of my teeth.

"There goes that stunning smile that stops everything for me."

I fixed my attention on him.

"Every fucking thing."

"Pryce, I can't help you," I whispered.

"You can more than you know."

"We both know you don't have an addiction to sex."

He shook his head. "No we don't."

"Yes we do." I placed my elbows on my desk and folded my hands. "If anything, you're just obsessed with pussy."

Why did I just say that?

He angled his hand at his crotch and grabbed the bulge forming there.

I licked my lips at it, then mentally kicked myself for reacting that way.

It was like the longer he stood before me, the more I forgot how to be professional in my own damn office.

"Don't say pussy around me, Dr. Waters." He smirked. "I'm trying to behave myself in here around you."

I balled my mouth to keep from laughing.

"Think about it," he offered. "'Cause I *need you*."

"You *need me*?"

"Your help," he corrected. "I *need* your help. Like for real, for real."

He approached my desk, and I leaned back against my chair. "You got my number. I know Marc already gave it to you."

I turned my head away to avoid his scent. It was enchanting and annoying, frustrating me and turning me on at the same time.

Ugh.

Pryce leaned in and took my chin gently between the pinch of his index and thumb fingers. His touch sent a zing between my legs that I had to clutch my thighs together to keep myself from jumping the man's bones in my place of business. I mean... we had the privacy.

"Call me when you're ready." He locked eyes with me and I couldn't stop myself from panting. "Aight?"

I said nothing when he backed away and made his way to my door, opening it and closing it behind him.

The moment he left, I dropped my head into my hands and tried my hardest to catch my breath.

I sat there for a few minutes longer, my eyes moving from my office door to everywhere around the room. I tried my hardest to understand how my day took the turn it did. With Pryce standing in my office, mere inches away from me, and I didn't feel the rage I thought I'd feel seeing him after all these years.

"Wow," I mumbled in my hands. "Did that really just happen?"

———

I turned into my father's driveway, my old driveway, and parked behind an 8-wheeler. In the shadows of Flatbush, the house and the neighborhood were like a secret hideaway. One turn off the public streets will have you driving down a stretch of land I like to call pleasant-ville.

Houses lined the block. Perfectly trimmed lawns resembled greenery photo'd for magazines. It was like Long Island in Brooklyn.

When I was younger, inviting friends over was always funny. Funny, because when they arrived, they'd all have the same shocked expression on their faces. You wouldn't know this area existed pacing along the outskirts of the community. This is what my father, Mr. Bernard Waters, loved - for his home to be a secret hideaway.

He and my mother bought the property when my sister was ten and

I only a few weeks old. It's been home ever since, even after I moved out after high school to attend college and never moved back in.

I put my silver *Benz* in park, unhooked my seatbelt and stepped out. My heels clicked against the concrete as I unbuttoned my blazer's buttons, peeling the jacket off me as I climbed the steps.

My father took excellent care of the house. A new white aluminum awning hung over the front door, and a quick peek at the porch swing's cushion showed he'd recently replaced it.

This was his thing these days after retiring, renovating his home. When he wasn't doing that, he busied himself working on engines and the like. My father was an independent truck driver. Which explained the 8-wheeler I parked behind in the driveway. But this truck wasn't his. He rented his truck out to companies interested in transporting goods across the states. On my father's free time, though, he fixed other truckers' trucks at a lower rate than the auto shops.

His third pastime was basketball, more specifically obsessing over the *Bronx Ballers*. He *adored* the team so much he got the *Bronx Ballers* logo tatted on his bicep when I was seven. He also used to collect *Bronx Ballers* memorabilia, a fact that smacked me right in the face the moment I pushed opened the house door.

"What in the cobwebbed hell is this?!" I questioned out loud.

My eyes landed on the couch the moment I stepped into the house. *Bronx Ballers* jerseys, hats, giant #1 foam fingers, team t-shirts in every color.

I approached the autographed framed poster of Peter Carter, one of the players that carried the *Bronx Ballers* to three finals in the 90s. In my hands, I examined the poster. There was dust all over the frame's glass.

"Ew." I placed it down and dusted my hands clean. "You got to be kidding me."

"Oh *he's* not," my sister, Gena, confirmed from the kitchen.

I made my way in that direction, stealing another glance at the *Bronx Ballers* swag, while shaking my head.

"What is happening in the living room and why?" I asked as I entered the kitchen.

"*What's happening* is your father's excitement for the resurgence of his most beloved team." She turned to me briefly. "Isn't it great! I have to see if the gray tee still fits."

"*Ugh*." I rolled my eyes. "I swear I can't stand the two of you sometimes."

Gena stood over the stove, stirring rice. Every other Friday we visited our father to catch up and to spend quality time together. Our careers took up a bulk of our workweeks and catching up on sleep from those careers snagged the remaining hours in a day. But Gena and I always stopped by the house to check up on our dad and to catch up.

"He pulled it out of the basement the moment he got wind that Pryce may play for the *Ballers* this fall."

"And who told him that?"

"It's common knowledge now." She beamed. "It's all over *ESPN*. Plus, I *might* have shared a *little* info the same night I heard it at the bar."

I sucked my teeth so hard I thought they'd shatter. "Why are y'all like this?"

"Oh, Leelah, stop it."

"Could y'all *please* be fans of another team and of another player? Damn. I don't get why that's so hard to do."

She blew raspberries with her lips.

"Anyway, where's dad?"

"Outside working on a truck." Gena spooned a little rice out of the pot and marched the spoon my way. "He's been waiting for you to get here to help him out."

"Of course." I sighed, glancing down at my painted nails that were chipping. "Thankfully I have a manicure appointment tomorrow."

I opened my mouth when Gena held the spoon in front of me. The moment the rice paired with andouille sausage and sautéed peppers touched my tongue, my taste buds lit up with flavor.

Gena took on the role of house cook after our mother passed away. G spent so much time in the kitchen with my mother growing up. She saved to memory most of our mother's recipes and could recreate them when our mother passed suddenly from cardiovascular disease. I was fourteen and Gena was twenty-four at the time. After our mother's passing, Gena refused to leave home until I did. She opted to attend

Langston University, then *New York University* for her PhD in computer science. Gena waited until I graduated high school to get her own place. She was like a second mother to me, a cool second mother who I told everything to, only because if I didn't she had a way with finding out, anyway.

I closed my eyes and indulged in the rice's taste on my tongue. "*Mmm.*"

"*Mm-hmm.* Good, huh?" She smiled from ear to ear. "Stole the recipe from Fenton."

"Fenton?!" I mewled as I chewed. "I'm surprised you haven't lost his number yet."

"He's kind of cool," she replied, placing the spoon in the sink. "Fenton likes to cook, I like to cook. He likes sports, I like sports."

I gasped and pointed at her. "You fucked him, didn't you?"

She twisted her lips to one side to keep from laughing. "He *knows* how to fuck, I *love* how he fucks."

I burst into laughter.

"Anyway..." I shook my head while swallowing the rest of my giggles. "Speaking of the *Bronx Ballers*... guess who showed up at the office today?"

Gena turned to face me with an arched brow. "*He* didn't."

"*He* sure did."

"Shut. Up!" Her jaw dropped. "You saw Pryce today?"

"Yup."

"Why didn't you lead with that? And you should have told me that before you got here. I would have brought vodka."

"I wish I did too because vodka is exactly what I need."

"*And,*" she added, "I would have brought my *Bronx Ballers* jersey for you to take with you to ask him to autograph."

I cocked my head to the right. "Gena!"

"What, La?" she whined. "Come on! Can't you be a little understanding about this?"

I folded my arms and balled my lips.

"Okay, fine, *fine*! My bad." She threw her hands up. "My supportive sister cape is back on and secured, promise."

"Thank you."

"So what happened?"

"I'll tell you later," I said, strolling toward the back door. "Let me go say hey to the old man."

"Okay, but I want to know *everything*."

I nodded and turned the knob to the backyard, stepping out.

Our house was built on a generous chunk of land. Back in the day, our dad would set up swing-and-slide play sets in the backyard space for us. It was like our own little park. These days, truck parts occupied the area along with my father on a plastic creeper laid up under a truck with only his long legs visible.

"Hey dad," I greeted as I approached.

He slid from under the truck with a smile. My father, Bernard Waters, had always been a big guy. Tall with a wide build, but he carried it well.

"Leelah!" He stood to his feet and pulled me into a hug.

I grimaced. "Dad, you have grease all over you."

"Aw, it ain't nothing." He hugged me tighter. "How you doin'?"

"Good, good." I closed my eyes and embraced him back. "I see you're working on something out here."

"*Mm-hmm.*" He stepped out of our hug and turned to gesture at the truck. "I got a guy who referred me to a trucker he met while on the road. Guy drove this thing all the way from *Pittsburgh* for me to work on. Needed new brakes, tires, and a filter change."

"Hmph."

"I need your help with changing the filter real quick."

I tilted my head to one side and pursed my lips.

"It'll be fast, you always do them so quick." He smiled. "Your hands have always moved faster than mine and they're so much smaller and graceful, making it easier for you to maneuver in those tight spots. No one can change a filter like my baby girl."

"But this isn't a car filter. It's a filter for a dirty old truck." I glanced down at my nails. "And you know I don't like to get my nails all dirty. That grease and dust will get all under my fingernails."

My father stared at me for a moment, his mouth set in a pout.

I rolled my eyes. "Do you have the cleaning solution to get all that gunk off my hands?"

"You know I always do."

I sighed. "Where are the new filters?"

A huge smile pulled at his lips as he turned to fetch them.

My dad taught me how to work on cars when I was nine. He'd always leave the truck work to only himself until I begged him to let me help when I was eleven. How trucks operated fascinated me. Everything was bigger on a truck and that was interesting to little me. While Gena was in the kitchen with our mother, I spent time outside with dad.

I stepped out of my heels, pulled the band from around my wrist and gathered my curls to the top of my head to secure in a messy bun. I stepped closer to the truck and climbed the short ladder to reach the engine's filter. Palmed the hand drill that sat on top of the closest tire. Pushing down on the nozzle to test the drill's speed, I placed the drill bit on the first screw to start removing the filter's cover.

"So...?" I asked as I worked. "What's up with the *Bronx Ballers* stuff in the living room?"

"I know you've heard."

"Did more than that." I drilled out the first screw and dropped it in my palm, then moved on to the other ones. "I saw the player himself."

My father's head whipped so fast in my direction I thought it would pop off.

"*You* saw Pryce?!"

"He stopped by my practice earlier today, unannounced."

"Oh, wow!" My father squatted into a seat on the grass in clear eye view. "What was his reason for stopping by?"

"Well, Marc called earlier this week asking me to see Pryce because Marc believes Pryce needs my professional help."

"Is that right?"

"Yeah." I sighed, pausing my work to look down at my dad to meet his eyes. "The thing is, I think they're both bullshitting me."

"What's bullshit about it?"

"Well, I can't say *why* he's there."

"Of course not." He agreed. "That's confidential."

"Right. It's just that, even if what Pryce needs my help with is a real thing, I don't know if I can help him."

"Because of y'all's past?"

"Exactly."

"That was high school Leelah, college for him."

I shook my head while returning my focus on the task at hand. "I wish everyone would stop telling me that."

"Well..." My father stood from his seat on the grass and approached, extending his hand so I'd drop the screws I removed from the filter's cover in his palm. "What does your heart tell you to do?"

"Help him."

"So go with your heart."

"But it's in a battle with my head." With all the screws removed, I pulled off the cover and coughed from the dust it dispersed. "Pryce put me in a bad headspace after we broke up. I went through several stages of grief that almost ruined my life, if I can be honest."

"Leelah—"

"Dad, just hear me out. I know he's like your favorite person in the world."

"Nonsense." My dad tapped my calf. "You know damn well you and your sister have *always* maintained that spot, your mother will forever too."

I smiled.

"Do I like Pryce? Yes, I do. He was a great guy to you, despite his eventual misstep."

I turned my eyes to face the exposed old filter, pulled it out, and dropped it to the grass. My father was quick to hand me the new engine filter which I positioned in place then slid in to its spot. "I don't want him to think he can waltz back into my life and we pick up where we left off because *he* wants to. I ended things with him. Shouldn't *I* be the one to initiate contact with him?"

My father released an audible exhale through his mouth. "I think you should meet up with him again."

I arched a brow.

"If for nothing else, to see where his head is at. And if you feel he really needs help, help the brother out."

"That's what my therapist told me," I replied, positioning the cover over the new filter. "Let me find out you're a natural born therapist." I drilled in the screws one at a time with the assistance of my father handing me each one.

"I think I've always given good advice." He grinned, handing me the last screw. "Where do you think you got your knack for it from?"

"I can't deny that." I wiggled my brows, my eyes focused on the gauge beside the cover. My final step was holding it down to reset the filter. "Well, I'm all done."

"See? What I tell you? It's like magic when you do it. Your hands move quick baby girl."

I stepped down the ladder and wrapped my arms tight around my father. "Thanks dad."

"No, thank you." He hugged me back. "Now when you meet up with him, let him know I'm real excited about him playing for the *Ballers*."

I leaned away a bit. "He hasn't even decided yet. From what I've read, it's only a rumor, he's said nothing about it."

"Speak it into existence for your dad."

I laughed out loud and so did he.

"Let's clean up and go inside before your big sister comes out here complaining that the food is getting cold."

"Let's," I replied while pushing my feet back into my heels one at a time.

As we made our way to his work shed next to the garage, I puffed my cheeks and blew the air out of my mouth slow, resolving to giving Pryce a call once I gathered enough courage to do so.

EIGHT

The bass from the hip hop track hummed from my speakers and played around me while I laid flat on my back in bed. My lights were off, but the glow from the skyscrapers through my window lit the room up enough to see. I drew opened the curtains that night for that specific reason.

Dressed in only my boxers, I ran my hand down my abs then buried my fingertips under the waistband as I scrolled through Leelah's *Instagram* profile.

She hadn't updated the thing in months. Her last picture was one she took on Christmas morning, capturing a Christmas tree with a few gifts underneath. The place looked familiar, like her father's house. I smiled as I kept scrolling, something I did on nights like this when I couldn't get her off my mind.

It had been five days since we seen each other in person for the first time in over a decade. The moment I laid eyes on her when she stepped out of her office and into the reception area, I thought I'd lose my discipline. I debated with myself on what I wanted to do more, pull her into a hug, kiss her, or ask her to marry me.

I laughed at the thought.

She'd gotten even more beautiful since I last saw her before moving out to Oakland. Her hair was a lot longer, and she wore it curly, a style she didn't wear back in the day. Lips were still full and pronounced at every angle, eyes still as gray as a cloudy day. I could still make her smile, which she did more than once. That was enough for me to think of another way to get in her presence. If pretending to need her help was something I needed to do to continue to close the distance between us, so be it. Even if it upset me to no end to do it.

My phone lit up with a call, and I furrowed my brows.

The number had a New York area code, but I wasn't familiar with it. No one had this number besides Marc and a few of my business associates, none of which lived in New York.

"Who dis'?" I answered.

"Hi," she purred on the other end.

I sat up in bed immediately. I'd saved her voice to memory, so I knew who it was instantly. "La?"

"Yeah."

My jaw dropped. I ran my hand down my mouth and swung my legs off the bed, jumping off it.

She called *me*.

My mind raced with what to say next. I didn't want to say anything that could end the call too quick.

She asked, "Are you still there?"

"Yeah, yeah... I'm just—"

"Shocked?"

"For lack of a better word, yes," I replied.

"Marc gave me this number," she breathed into the phone. "I hope it's okay."

"Hearing your voice on the other end of my phone? It's more than okay."

She was quiet.

"Are you smiling right now?"

"Maybe."

I bit down on my bottom lip and nodded. "Good."

She exhaled a sexy giggle. I grew stiff in my boxers, reactively.

"Listen," she began, "the reason I'm calling you is to invite you out to dinner."

My brows shot up.

"You said you needed my help and I think there are some things we need to get out of the way before we can move to the step of us working together on your addiction."

I shut my eyes and clenched my jaw. Nothing pissed me off more than Marc making that shit up. Not the fact that it wasn't true, but that I had to lie to Leelah, which I really didn't want to do. But it was like he said, there was no way she would see me if he hadn't lied. Hell, the only reason she was calling me was because she believed I needed her help.

"Pryce, are you still there?"

"Yeah, yeah, I'm here. Um..." I scratched the back of my head. "Let's do that. Dinner sounds like a plan. When did you have in mind?"

———

We settled on Friday night at nine. *GrayArea* restaurant, bar and lounge was the place we made plans to meet. I was the first to arrive. It was my intention to arrive fifteen minutes before we agreed to, so I could see her walk in.

Waiting the two days to link up wrecked my nerves. I was anxious to see her again. Even contemplated being outright honest with her about Marc's bullshit lie concerning me having a sex addiction, but thought that wouldn't be the right move.

Before my arrival, I picked up 30 stems of calla lilies. They laid on the table in front of the spot she would sit with a red ribbon wrapped tight around the stems forming a bow. I noticed she had similar flowers sitting in a vase on her coffee table in her office. Figured they must be her favorite now, so I brought a bunch with me to give her during dinner.

I glued my eyes to the door, so I'd see her the moment she walked in, and when she did, everything around her blurred.

All I could see was her.

Tonight she had on a simple black bandeau dress. The fabric hugged her from her breasts to a few inches above her knees. On top of it, she wore a black blazer with slim sleeves.

Shorty had always been a siren to me, even before she knew she was. Thick build, breasts that spilled out of whatever she wore, undefined but naturally cinched waist, and a pair of hips and ass that could be seen from every angle. Her first week in *Turner High School*, I took notice of her. Leelah's body was the first thing I saw, and once I got past her curves and made eye contact with her, I had to have her.

She was only a few feet closer when one of my security guards left their corner to approach.

"She's good," I announced, as I stood up, making my way over to her chair.

"They were ready to take me out, huh?" she joked. "You would think they weren't at my office not long ago, crowding my reception area."

"Nah, you good, you good."

"You're on time," she noted when she arrived at our table.

"I don't believe in being late."

"Never have." She smiled. "One of the few people I know who has so much respect for time."

We stared at each other for a moment before she glanced down at the table. Her face lit up with a smile.

"Are these for me?"

"Yes they are."

"Beautiful." She balled her lips to get rid of her smile, but that didn't work because it only grew bigger. "Calla lilies are my favorite."

"I figured." I reached behind her to pull out her chair. My forearm grazed the back of her blazer when she shivered. I licked my lips at her reaction. She was still sensitive to touch. That was a very insightful reminder.

Leelah took a seat and removed her blazer, putting the girls, her cleavage, right in my view.

"I debated with myself on if this dress was appropriate," she voiced.

"*GrayArea* doesn't have a dress code," I told her as I took a seat across from her.

"Appropriate for *you*."

"Me?"

"Yeah, my cleavage and your addiction don't mix."

I balled my hands into fists and released them.

That damn Marc.

"Nah, you good."

For the next few minutes we reviewed the menu in silence. Once we decided what we wanted to eat and sip on, our focus landed on each other.

"Gena and my dad send their regards."

"Oh yeah?" I smiled. "That's what's up. How have they been?"

"Well, G is a Senior Tech at an IT firm on Park Ave."

"Nice!"

"And my dad retired from trucking," she answered with a nod. "Now, he works on other people's trucks and just pulled out old *Bronx Ballers* memorabilia from the deep recesses of the basement."

I lifted my fist to my lips and laughed into it.

"Because," she continued through her giggles, "he's convinced, well, the both of them, that you will play for the *Ballers* come October."

"Wow, that's dope."

"He became a pseudo-*Flames* fan the moment news broke you signed with them."

"Oh word?" I replied. "Well, that's dope, too. For real."

"Gena's been loyal to the *Ballers* since forever though." She bit at the side of her bottom lip nervously. "Is it true?"

"Is what true?"

"That you're thinking about signing with them? The *Bronx Ballers*?"

I lifted, then dropped my shoulders. "I'm unsure at the moment. That all depends."

"On?"

"Things. Future commitments." I locked my eyes with hers. "Present company included."

She jerked her head back. "Wh-what's that supposed to mean?"

Our waitress with the help of a server returned to our table with our food and drinks, and they left just as quickly.

We were quiet for a moment, Leelah's eyes focused down on her plate, body motionless.

An awkward silence fell over the table. I feared I was too forward. Maybe I should have played that card later in the night, much later in the night, in fact. The card that revealed my motive to change teams... her.

I reached for my snifter full of brandy and took a large nervous gulp.

"You can't just do that," she blurted.

I met my eyes with hers.

"Break my heart, leave, then barge back in my life when you want to. Who told you, you could do that?"

"*You* broke up with *me*."

"*You* cheated on *me*!" she hollered. She pressed her hand to her chest and glanced around herself. Leelah shut her eyes tight. She took a breath before opening her eyes and focusing on me again.

"So..." I placed my glass down. "We're *not* gonna eat first, huh?"

"If you need my help, I can help you." Her eyes widened, gray eyes becoming stormy with tears. "But if you're aiming for anything else, Pryce, and I mean *anything else*, you can just forget it because you *won't* get it. That is not an option."

The stinging that pierced my heart made me grit my teeth. I had to take a quick breath and keep focus though. She was right, but I needed this. I needed her.

"And why not?" I quizzed. "*Why* is *that* not an option?"

"What?"

"I mean... hypothetically, if this were more than needing your help, why couldn't I have that?"

"Why couldn't you have that?!" She challenged. "Do you have any idea how long it took me to get past what you did?"

I lifted my glass of brandy to my lips and sipped. My attempt at calming my heart that pounded in response to the grief in her eyes was failing horribly.

"Way too long." She shook her head. "Life changed a lot for me after the night we broke up, Pryce. My perspective on things became warped as fuck."

"You were innocent, and I'm sorry." I leaned forward in my chair and lowered my voice. "I'm *really* sorry. It's important you understand that."

"Innocent?" She questioned. "Now that's something I haven't been in a while."

I squinted my eyes at her.

"You know... after I ended things with you," she began. "I fell into a depression I was in denial about. Senior year, I gained sixteen pounds, skipped prom, and I almost didn't go to graduation because none of that mattered to me. You were my entire world and when you did what you did and we broke up, and you left New York, I was just... like... fuck it. Fuck, everything. Like a fool, I shaped my identity, my future plans, my everything on *you* while we were together. I realized years later that was more my fault than yours. Investing so much energy into a relationship, into intimacy, so young and not even spending half that energy on myself. I realized my error with you way too late though."

She reached for her wine and took a long sip of it.

"Then came college." She took a gulp shortly after the sip and forced a short laugh. "If I didn't have my head in a textbook, I had someone's son's head between my thighs."

"What the fuck did you just say?!" I said through my teeth, but low enough for only us to hear.

My jaw tightened as I lowered my chin to my chest to keep from losing my shit in there.

She wore an expression that was somewhere between a smirk and a sneer. Leelah was clearly satisfied with my reaction.

"You heard exactly what I said. Like an even bigger fool, I went searching for you in other guys," she continued. "Searching for the best parts of you, at least. And most of them didn't enjoy talking much, so I figured, give them a little pussy to get a little affection or maybe bits of their personalities that reminded me of you. I really didn't have the time for anything else, anyway."

I looked away, running my hand down my beard, trying but again failing to take in even breaths.

"Lost count after nine."

I twisted my head back in her direction quick.

"A lot of them, I don't even remember their names. I could stroll right past the others and not glance twice because honestly, I wouldn't even recognize them by face."

The voices in the restaurant swelled in volume, and so did my heartbeats as my heart tried its best to pound out of my chest.

"And I always had hope, you know?" she revealed. "That maybe this one will be like Pryce, the best parts of him minus the cheating. Maybe *this* guy will give me that thing I can't name but would remember what it felt like once I felt it again."

I tossed back the rest of my brandy and let the drink sear down my throat.

"But I always slinked away, embarrassed, dissatisfied, and disappointed. An *insatiable appetite* is what one guy chastised me for having. They could never give me what I wanted. So three became five, five ballooned to nine, and finally I found no use in continuing to count. Until..." She held up a finger for emphasis. "... I came to my senses and realized what I was running around here searching for just didn't exist anymore—"

"That's a lie, 'cause I'm right here," I jumped in. "*I'm*. Right. Here. You were searching for *me*? For something I made you feel? Well, come get it. I'm back. Right here in your face. Come and get *me,* La."

She shook her head. "I made my commitment to chastity and will only break that vow for the man who's worth breaking it for. I had to force myself into chastity two years ago to save me *from* me. So, yeah, *you're* here now, but your innocent Leelah is long gone."

"Nah, she right here with me." I squeezed my thumb in my palm to keep cool. Tears pricked at the sides of my eyes. I couldn't remember a time I'd been so pissed off with a situation... or with *myself*. Losing everything I owned wouldn't bring on this type of anger, this breadth of pain. No, this anger hurt and cut deep. I was bleeding out inside. Took everything in me to keep from knocking everything off the table, ripping all the shit in the room to shreds to get out the rage coursing through me from her truth that maimed my ego. Instead, I just sat still and focused on her.

It was killing me slowly knowing, in my absence, she'd shared herself with fools who didn't deserve that side of her. But still, I had to let her know that, "I don't give a fuck about who you were with after me 'cause they don't matter."

She pushed her tongue against her cheek and looked away. When she blinked, the tears she'd been holding back slid down her face and my heart ached at the sight of it all.

"I've done some shit, too," I confessed. "You don't remember their names? I don't even remember sleeping with the few women who claim

I did. And the number? Nowhere near nine, so I'm in no position to judge."

"Don't give me that," she spat through her teeth. "Don't even try it. I know you well enough to know that *to you*? It is not the same, so please."

"You right." I swallowed hard. "You're so right, but I meant what I said. I *don't care* Leelah. You ain't give none of those niggas your heart, and I didn't give any of those women I fucked with after you mine."

She focused on me, her chest heaving hard, more tears falling.

"La." I pushed my chair back to stand up and take her in my arms, but she stopped me by holding her hand up.

"*Don't.*" She brought her hands to her face and covered her eyes, exhaling audibly in defeat. "I can't do this with you. I can't help you, I can't be here. This was a mistake. I'm sorry."

"Leelah."

"I have to go."

"Please," I pleaded. "Leelah..."

Before I could reach for her, she pushed her chair back, stood up, snatched her blazer and bag off the back of the chair and stormed off toward the exit.

"Fuck!" I yelled, slamming my fist down on the table and watching the dishes, silverware, and glasses rattle.

All eyes were on me as people twisted their heads my way or turned in their seats to face me.

"Boss?" Kyle, one of my security guards, called as he took steps toward me.

I held my hand up.

"I'm good, I'm good," I assured him.

But I was far from that. Instead, I was slowly running out of time... and faith.

NINE

I balanced myself at the edge of my bed, the arches of my feet propped up against my white furry area rug. I wrapped my fingers around my phone, my teeth biting the side of my lip.

After storming out of the restaurant, I caught a cab and came straight home, then jumped in the shower, hoping to wash away any remnants of defeat.

I told myself before arriving to dinner with Pryce that I would play it cool. The whole time - when I arrived, sat at the table, ordered our food and drinks - I was nervous. Then when he alluded to his decision to sign with the *Ballers* having something to do with me, I misplaced my cool entirely.

What did he even mean it depends? What was conditional?

The uncertainty made me uneasy. His audacity, too. Who told him he had the right to decide when he could make another reentry into my life in any capacity? That's supposed to be *my* call.

I dropped my forehead into my free hand and exhaled air through my mouth. Just sitting in my room recalling our conversation was bringing back a lot of the same emotions I experienced sitting across from him in that restaurant. Still, I had an obligation. As a psychotherapist, turning my back on Pryce without even referring him elsewhere would be unethical... even though I couldn't shake the belief that his sex addiction was bullshit. But I also couldn't shake the thought that I might have felt that way because of my distrust of him after he broke my heart.

I mean, what the hell else did he want from me if not my professional help, anyway? He had the fame, the money, a particular lifestyle. Pryce could have his pick of any woman he wanted. I've seen the women he's been with after me, the entire world has. Models, cover girls, actresses photo'd on his tatted arm. He couldn't possibly want *me* back... could he?

I shook my question out of my head and bounced my legs on the arches of my feet.

I'll admit. That moment in the restaurant, when I revealed my body count, gave me some level of satisfaction. It was clear me telling him that hurt him and that pleased me. What man wanted to imagine the girl who he once believed to be as pure as silk performing not so pure acts with other men?

I sighed, peeking down at my phone.

But I had to show him I wasn't just sitting around watching paint dry, allowing my life to pass me by like some dreaded slideshow. I needed him to know he wasn't the only one moving on with life and that all this time; I wasn't waiting for him... even though I kind of was.

I kissed my teeth and unlocked my device, then tapped into my phone app. My thumb hovered over his name for three beats. Finally, I tapped on it to place the call.

The phone rang once before Pryce answered. "La?"

"I'm sorry," I apologized with more breath than tone. "I shouldn't have left like that."

"It's aight," he replied. "You don't have to apologize."

"Yes, I do." I sighed. "You asked for my help and I let personal shit get in the way. That wasn't my intention tonight when I invited you out for dinner."

He said nothing.

"*We* were years ago and that should not affect the work we need to do for your healing today... that's if you still want my help."

"Uh, yeah," he voiced, uncertainty laced in his tone which I attributed to what happened at the restaurant between us. "I need you." Pryce cleared his throat. "Your help, I need your help."

"Okay," I whispered, leaning back in my seat and folding my legs. "I want you to come in to my office for an evaluation. When are you next free?"

He exhaled into the phone. "Wednesday will probably work best for me."

I moved the phone away from my ear, placed it on speaker, and clicked out of the phone app and into my calendar app. "How does 2 p.m. sound?"

"Good," he replied. "I can head there after the gym."

"Okay, so 2 p.m. on Wednesday. I'll block it out and will have my secretary add it to my main calendar on Monday."

"Cool."

The both of us remained on the line for a moment, silent, just listening to each other breathe.

"You have to be sexually abstinent," I spoke into the phone.

There was another brief moment of silence before he asked, "I'm sorry, absti-what?"

A laugh bellowed from my mouth before I had sense to stop it. "Pryce, you heard me."

"Abstinent for *what*?!"

"A part of the treatment requires that you refrain from sex. So, you have to practice sexual abstinence once we begin."

"You *cannot* be serious."

I stifled my laugh by tucking my lips into my mouth. "We'll talk more about it on Wednesday."

He scoffed.

"Try to keep an open mind about this. I know women throw themselves at you every day—"

"I don't care about none of that," he interjected. "All I care about is you—" He inhaled sharply.

"Me? What about me?"

"If you need me to be celibate, or abstinent, or whatever it is that you're asking for me to be," he redirected, "then I can be that, I guess. Maybe. I can at least try... I think."

My eyes darted around the room, brows furrowed as I tried to make sense of his previous comment that should have been so obvious to me in that instance. "Okay. So... Wednesday."

"Yeah, Wednesday," he confirmed.

The moment we ended the call, I fell back on the bed and trained my eyes on my ceiling.

I blew raspberries with my lips. "I *really* hope I know what I'm doing here with this man."

With the phone still in my grip, I rolled over and onto my belly with an idea that made sense at the time. My eyes were on the screen when I clicked into my Safari app to Google *Pryce Williams*. Before I could press search after typing in his name, suggested search terms popped up. ***Pryce Williams's age***, ***Pryce Williams's height***, ***Pryce Williams's stats***, ***Pryce Williams sex tape***.

I furrowed my brows at the last search term and went right for the bait.

Freeze frames of Pryce in action appeared in the images. News stories covering the situation populated the page, too.

I remembered vaguely the sex tape being big talk three years ago. Everyone raved about it, most notably the size of his dick.

I snickered to myself. That thing always scared me before we were intimate. I was familiar with Pryce's anatomy long before the sex. We did a few things before actually making love, and to say Pryce was more than a mouthful would be an understatement.

There was a website claiming to have the tape in its entirety.

I bit at my lip as I contemplated clicking the link to watch.

"He's a new client," I told myself, nodding my reassurance. "This is just research. I'm only watching this for research."

I tapped into the site, then pressed play on the video. The action pulled me in immediately.

The moans of his partner were the most audible. She held the recording device, but with all the movement and the fog clouding the lens, the view was blurry. Not blurry enough to hide Pryce's face.

He had his bottom lip tucked in his mouth, pinned by the bite of his teeth. I remembered that look. When he was deeply invested in his work, totally enraptured by the moment. Just the sight of his expression did something to me I couldn't control even if I tried.

"*Ahh*," she moaned. "It's too much, baby."

"*Mmm*, not for you though, right?" He groaned out.

She pressed a hand to his abs, and he responded by pumping his pelvis forward, gradually increasing his speed.

"Nah, don't fold on me," he told her through breaths. "Show me you can handle me."

I rolled my eyes and clicked out of the website, tossing the phone on the bed.

My breaths escaped my body heavy. I tried to control them, but it was no use. I wish I could say the little I watched pissed me off or hurt me, but it did the opposite. The video actually turned me on.

Reclining flat on the bed, I brought my hand between my thighs and glided my fingers down the fabric of my panties.

"No." I snatched my hands away and shut my eyes to gather myself. "Do *not*."

The second I closed my eyes though, I saw his sex face, his lip tucked between his teeth. The measured movements of his torso as he stroked in and out of whoever that woman was, kept flashing through my mind. It was so vivid, attractive, and unfortunately a huge turn on.

Why was it such a turn on?!

Maybe it was because it was only him captured in the scene I watched. Yeah, whatever woman was there with him, but only in voice. In view was just Pryce. Stroking, sweating, muscles flexing and torso moving with such skill, reminding me of a man who was once mine and who did things to my body no man had been able to replicate after him.

I shut my eyes again to clear my mind of it, of him. But as hard as I tried, getting his face and his hip movements out of my head seemed like a losing battle. I didn't even watch the video for a full minute and my mind was left in shambles.

So for the first time in two years, I gave myself three orgasms with him in mind before drifting off to sleep.

TEN

Her space was quiet, the city just outside her window. Leelah's SoHo office wasn't the busiest spot in NYC, but it had its share of foot traffic.

Yet, you wouldn't be privy to that sitting in the armchair only feet away from her desk. At least I couldn't sense anything outside these four walls.

I watched her pull out a small yellow notepad, observing as she turned the hourglass on her desk to the opposite side. The sand from one end poured into the other, drawing my attention to the two connected glass bulbs.

"You don't believe in using clocks?" I asked.

She smiled.

"I like to go a little old school in my sessions." Leelah pointed at the hourglass. "This takes exactly 45-minutes for the sand to sift to the opposite side, making it enough time for the evaluation today."

"And what's this evaluation for?"

"To see if you need treatment, if I can help you."

I sighed. "I didn't know I would take a test."

"It's not a test, Pryce," she explained. "It's an assessment. I want to help you, but that's not the same as me *being able* to help you. What we

want to do often differs with what we can do. So this is an assessment to
see if the help you need is what *I* can provide, okay?"

I nodded my understanding.

"I mean... *if* you even have a sex addiction at all."

Our eyes met, and hers bored into mine. She looked at me differently. The last time we saw each other at the restaurant, our final few
minutes together at least, she appeared broken. Like I'd picked at an
old scab that hadn't yet healed. Today, there was no angry glare in her
eyes.

Leelah shifted her attention away when our eyes stayed locked for
too long.

"Okay." She folded over a page on her yellow notepad. "I will ask you
a few questions and I want you to answer honestly."

"Aight."

"When was the last time you watched porn?"

"I don't watch. I prefer to make my own."

"I've seen," she mumbled as she scribbled words on her pad, or at
least I think I heard her say that.

I arched a brow. "I'm sorry, what was that?"

"Moving on," she continued, "And when was the last time you
masturbated?"

"Three nights ago."

She peeked up at me, then dropped her eyes to her notepad to write
something again.

"And the last time you had sex?"

"Two weeks ago."

"Two weeks ago?" she questioned. "And you haven't had sex since?"

I shook my head.

"Was she your girlfriend?"

I shook my head again. "Nah, they were just acquaintances."

"*They*?"

"Yeah."

"More than one?"

"Yes."

"How many?"

"Two."

"Okay." Her eyes returned to her notepad. "Same day, correct? Like, within hours?"

"Same time," I corrected. "Like, one after the other."

She lifted her eyes to mine, her brows arched high above them

I shrugged a shoulder. "It was a light night."

Her jaw dropped before she forced her mouth closed.

"Hmm..." She adjusted her position in her chair as her pupils returned on her notepad to jot more down. "Usually someone has to have sex in some way every day to sustain an addiction. They can't function without it. You don't watch porn, you're not masturbating regularly..."

Fuck, I knew I should've Googled this shit.

"I got to be honest with you."

"Okay...?"

"Sex addiction is a tricky focus for me. People's addictions to sex are usually deeper issues masked by the coping mechanism of needing to fuck away our problems."

"Dr. Waters." I pressed my palm to my chest, faking surprise. "Is this how you talk to your other clients?"

"All the time. That's why they like me so much." She smirked. "I don't sugarcoat, which is why I have to be real with you and inform you that sex therapy will force you into the missionary position if you don't really have an addiction. Regular sex is healthy. Actually, lack of it, if you aren't celibate, is viewed as a problem by some psychologists. The work done here will help you learn how to keep your sexual urges from controlling you instead of you learning how to control them. That is, *if...*" She hissed a little on that "f." "... you really have a sex addiction."

That damn Marc.

I ran my palm down my face slow and over the length of my beard.

"The reason I agreed to help was because if you do have a sex addiction, I suspect your addiction is psychological and stems from your involvement with Renee. Then there's your abandonment by your mother."

I jerked my head back. "My mother? Renee? How you figure?"

"Well, your relationship with Renee was highly unconventional and far from healthy. She was a twenty-something year old woman engaging in sex with you, her teenage next-door neighbor. You might not have seen a problem with it back then, but that was abuse."

Renee was a woman who taught me all about sex. I was always a big kid, at least six feet before starting high school. Grains of facial hair had already sprouted when she invited me to her crib one afternoon after school. I lived with my father, who worked the graveyard shift as a security guard in a high rise in the city. My mother dipped when I was five and I hadn't seen her until I was drafted fifteen years later and she conveniently was ready for a relationship with her son. Suffice to say, I had no real adult supervision as a teenager. Renee initiated our sexual relationship when I was 14 by inviting me over one afternoon and giving me head in her kitchen. Oral sex soon progressed to her riding my dick on her couch after school. She was a sexy woman, didn't at all look like she was in her late twenties. And at my 14-years of age, I of course was gamed for whatever she was gamed for. I considered myself lucky to be involved with a woman like her. She was older and could have whatever nigga she wanted, but she wanted me. That shit did wonders for my teenage ego and confidence. We fucked with each other off and on, on the low, until I was seventeen. That was the year I laid eyes on Leelah.

"Who the fuck is this little girl you running around here with?" Renee snapped on me one afternoon in her living room.

"She's my girlfriend," I replied.

"Your what?! Since when?"

"Since last month."

She gritted her teeth. "How can you have a girlfriend if you're with me?"

I grimaced. "We ain't together though. You told me that yourself."

"Well you gotta break up with her." Renee folded her arms. "There's no way she can do for you what I'm doing. She probably don't even fuck yet. The girl look like she's one year shy of 12-years-old. What the hell are you doing with her, Pryce?!"

The two would eventually meet one day after school when Renee showed up outside the gates of our high school. Her popping up with no warning was the first time I realized how crazy women could really get. Renee and I stopped sexing the day I made things official with Leelah. Her antics outside my school forced me to stop talking to her altogether and to tell Leelah all about the relationship Renee and I had. The funny thing is, Leelah never looked at me differently because of my relationship with Renee. She listened and of course wasn't cool with Renee and my involvement, but Leelah never judged me. That was the day I knew Leelah was the one because of her understanding and refusal to judge.

"Addiction takes root in the reward center of the brain," Leelah informed, pulling me back in the moment with her. "When we orgasm, our mid-brain, the section of the brain that handles our body's reward system and survival, activates. Sex creates a rush of dopamine, a feel-good chemical in our brain. Dopamine triggers feelings dealing with pleasure. An obsession with that hormonal release and the escape it offers is what leads to addiction."

I licked my lips slow at her then bit my bottom lip. She did not understand how hearing her talk like this turned me on.

"Do you have sex on your mind right now?"

"As a matter of fact, yes, I do." I leaned forward in my seat and she leaned back in hers. "I'm thinking about sex with you."

She blinked her eyes in response.

"I'm thinking about you and your desk." I licked my lips. "You on your desk, on this couch, and on me." I pointed. "Shit, even on the chair you're sitting on. I'm sure I can make do with the small space the chair provides."

Leelah swallowed hard, her chest rising and falling.

I smirked to myself, pleased with knowing I could still arouse her with only my words. So I proceeded. Fuck all these formalities.

"Do you know that after all these years, I can still remember how your pussy tastes?"

She slacked her jaw, then exhaled and inhaled through her mouth.

"I don't think I could ever forget, honestly," I added.

"Um..." She pinched the innermost corners of her eyes. "How often do you think of sex with other women?"

"And your moan," I continued despite her attempt to change focus. "I'll never forget it either. You always had the sexiest moan. Especially when I went deep. You always loved when I refused to hold back with you. Find your spot and refuse to let up off it."

"Okay, *no*," she purred, damn near moaned before clearing her throat and sitting up in her seat. "Pryce... you can't talk like that to me."

"You asked."

"You *can not* talk to me like that."

"In here?" I smirked. "Or period?"

She exhaled a nervous laugh, then brought her hand to her eyes to blindfold them.

I couldn't help but to smile at her reaction. This was unprofessional for sure but let's be real here, this addiction shit was bullshit, at least it was for me. Yeah, my mother leaving was fucked up and the shit I did with Renee, as I see it now, was fucked up too, but I didn't have any hang ups over neither of them, to my knowledge. I had to get Leelah out of that headspace somehow though, and fast.

"Cognitive-behavioral therapy will work for you."

Dammit.

"I've tried it with other clients with success. It's the most commonly used treatment for sex addiction because I direct my focus on identifying triggers for addictive behavior."

I stared at her, wondering if I were to stand up from my seat and approach her desk would she let me. If I pulled her into a kiss, would she fight me on it?

"I'll teach you skills to cope with those triggers once we identify them."

On this day, she wore this form-fitting orange dress. The neckline scooped down, offering just a peek at her cleavage, much different from the last time I showed up at her office. I assumed she pulled on this dress for me, in an attempt to not *trigger* me. But she could wear a potato sack, and I'd still see her naked in my mind.

"Pryce?"

"Yeah?"

"Stop it."

"I can't." A smile pulled at my lips. "My addiction, remember?"

"You will make me end this session sooner than I'd like."

"You should probably go 'head and end it then because I'm unsure of how much longer I'll be able to control myself alone in here with you."

She tried to fight her smile, but lost.

"Orange is definitely your color baby."

She directed her gaze away shyly.

My smile melted off my lips. "But seriously, I'm sorry for hurting you La."

She jerked her head in my direction.

"I'm making it clear that my attraction to you is still very real but I don't want you mistaking this for something only physical, because it isn't. It's much more. *We* were much more. So I'm sorry, and I mean that from the heart."

She moved her head up and down. "Since we're being honest and speaking from the heart..."

"Yeah?"

"Based on your responses, I have doubts you're a sex addict. You could benefit from therapy to heal your past emotional traumas, but this claim of sex addiction is throwing me off. I hate to say it out loud, but I suspect you're bullshitting me. It just isn't clear why yet. I'm going against my better judgement right now and honestly going further than I would like in here with you. As a therapist, I would hate to turn a patient away who really needs my help, especially someone I know personally. And like I told you, given your history with Renee, your claim of addiction *does* hold validity. But... I just..." She squinted her eyes at me. "I don't know."

I shifted my eyes away from hers. The part of me wanting to admit the truth battled with the other side of me, needing desperately for her to trust me again. Marc throwing this monkey wrench of a sex addiction into the mix threw my game off, but I wasn't about to tell her the truth, not right now at least.

"Anyway, this is the end of the evaluation. When you leave, I'll review your responses and will call you regarding if I can take you on as a client or if I'll need to refer you to someone else."

I clapped my hands together once and stood to my feet. "Cool."

Her eyes followed me as I made my way to the office door.

"And La?"

"Yes?"

"You can call me for other things besides letting me know if you can take me on as a client or not."

She pressed the tip of her tongue against the inside of her cheek. "And why on earth would I ever do that?"

"Aren't doctors always on-call for their patients?"

"For their patients to call them," she corrected. "Not for them to call patients."

"Well, feel free to break protocol for me. I won't mind it at all."

We stared at each other for a moment longer before I winked at her and walked out, closing the door behind me.

ELEVEN

Midnight struck when I lowered the rim of my wine glass away from my lips. The session I had earlier in the day with Pryce was intense. Before his arrival, it wasn't clear what type of meeting we would have when things between us were still up in the air.

In the time we sat in my office, he hadn't convinced me he was an addict, although he played the part well. I'd been around enough addicts to notice the telltale signs. But I couldn't deny him my services. I mean, I *could*, but I didn't want to. Besides my conscience getting the best of me and influencing my need to do the right thing, being in Pryce's company again made me feel... good.

I lifted the bottle of Bordeaux and poured it into the wineglass, filling the glass to the top. I was three glasses in and my thoughts still hadn't offered clarity. In fact, they got even cloudier.

I wondered what he was doing at that hour. Was he entertaining another woman? Perhaps two of them? Three?

I pinched the space between my eyes when the intimate scene from his sex tape faded in to memory.

Since the night I relieved myself, after viewing only a few minutes of his sex tape, I'd masturbated every night thereafter. I'd taken a vow of abstinence, or what I'd like to consider a vow of chastity, with myself. Had this ceremony with just me in attendance, where I meditated on the decision and signed an agreement with myself. So damn melodramatic. But the plan was to remain chaste, no sex or even self-pleasure since in the past, masturbating always acted like a gateway that led to me sleeping with men I shouldn't sleep with. I planned to remain chaste until I found the right person to break the vow I made to myself. But slowly my chastity vow was fading between my fingers.

I wanted him and I realized how much I wanted him when he swaggered into my office earlier that day dressed in workout gear. The shirt he wore laid snug against his chest, arms bulging, tats visible. His gray sweatpants outlined his dick so well he should've just stumbled in there with the waistband at his ankles.

I sighed and gulped the wine, finishing yet another glass.

My head was light, thoughts still heavy. I glanced at my phone lying on my counter and bit inside my lip. His suggestion of me calling him for other things echoed from the corners of my mind. I couldn't do that and still take him on as a client.

How stupid and careless would that be?

I shook my head while rubbing my lips together. In another breath, I scooped up my device and tiptoed to my en-suite bathroom to wash away the workday with a focus on climbing in bed to retire for the night.

An hour later, cleansed, moisturized and half a glass short of being drunk, I pressed my back to my headboard and stared up at my wooden barrel ceilings. The street lamps lit up my loft from the outside, shadows of trees and their leaves left temporary tattoos on my floors and walls. The wooden columns holding up the ceilings resembled tall guards in the dark. I wished they could shield me from what I couldn't stop thinking to do.

I've lived in this loft for the past five years. Bought it when the real estate market was lukewarm for loft sales and agreed to buy the loft at a more than generous price. It was a raw, open space, practically everything made of authentic wood the way I preferred it. My favorite were the large warehouse-like paned windows I often stood in front of to people-watch pedestrians passing by below my view. Elevated over my kitchen and living area was my room, a room that felt lonely at the moment.

I glanced at my vanity table where my phone laid and rolled off the bed to retrieve it.

Red wine coursed through my veins, giving me an audacity that had no business being there. In bed and with my phone in hand, I clicked into my phone app and scrolled down to Pryce's number. I'd called him five days prior, so his phone number was still fresh in my call log.

Like the last time, the line only rang once before he answered.

"What's good, La?"

His voice was rasped with exhaustion.

I shut my eyes tight, already regretting the call.

"Were you sleeping?"

"Don't matter?" he replied. "I'm up now."

I slid my tongue below my top lip and exhaled into the phone.

"It's late," I whispered. "I shouldn't be calling you."

"Then why did you call me?"

"Because I've had too much wine and I'm clearly not thinking straight."

He chuckled. "Drinking on a school night, Dr. Waters?"

I giggled.

"You still have the sexiest laugh," he told me.

My smile melted off my lips. We sat silently on the line for what seemed like forever until Pryce asked...

"What you looking for right now, La?"

"I don't know." I wedged the phone between my head and shoulders, as I lowered down onto my pillow. The moment my head touched the surface of the cushion, I slid my fingertips south between my thighs. "I'm... conflicted."

A gust of air pushed through my nose and vibrated through the phone the second the pads of my fingers made contact with my clit.

"You aight over there?"

"*Mm-hmm*," I answered, my fingers circling the tip of my pink pearl.

"'Cause you sound... *busy*."

"My hand is between my legs," I whispered into the phone, closing my eyes. "I'm playing with myself."

"Wait, *what*?" Bedsheets rustled on the other end of my phone before Pryce said, in a deeper voice, "What did you just say?"

A moan escaped through my lips. I'd stroked a sensitive spot. My walls contracted reactively.

"Oh *shit*," he whispered. Pryce released two quick exhales into the phone. "You for real right now?"

"*Mm-hmm.*" I picked up the speed. "We can forget this ever happened, but right now I just need you to just talk to me."

"Baby," he replied with haste. "I can do more than just *talk* to you. Tell me where you are."

"*Uh-uh.*" I moaned again as my job became easier thanks to my juices lubricating my play.

"Fuck, girl." He groaned. "What are you doing right now to me?"

"I watched a little of your sex tape," I confessed, never stopping my hand movements.

"So I heard you correctly in your office earlier when you said you'd seen it?" he asked. "Did you like it? Is that what's got you like this right now?"

"That and what you told me earlier." I clutched my thighs around my wrist, moved the phone off my ear, and put it on speaker. "About what you'd do to me."

"I meant that," he promised. "I meant every last word and I can come over right now and do all the shit I told you I'd do and more if you tell me where you are."

"No, uh-uh. I'm not even supposed to be doing this, and definitely not with *yooouuu*!"

A spike of pleasure crawled through, causing goosebumps to sleeve my limbs.

He grunted. "La *please* tell me where you at."

"Did you want me earlier today?" I panted. "Because I wanted you."

"You wanted me? Are you for real?" Pryce's voice went up two octaves. "Yo, is this the wine?!"

Another moan escaped my lips.

"*Damn*," he exhaled in a strained voice. "Fuck it. I don't even give a shit if this is just the wine talkin'. You should've told me this earlier, Leelah. You know all you had to do was say the word and you know I would've given you *everything* you wanted."

My back arched off the bed when the first wave of my climax approached. "This is wrong."

"Yeah, because I'm over here and you're over there fucking with me *without* me. Quit playing and tell me where you are, woman!"

"You were right," I continued. "I've always liked it deep. I loved when you put all of you inside of me."

"La, I swear to God—"

"And your kisses." I licked my lips. "I can still taste them."

A groan echoed from my phone's speaker. "How about my dick, huh? You remember what that taste like too?"

"*Mm-hmm,*" I answered. "And your cum."

He growled a moan into the phone in response.

"Are you touching yourself?" I asked.

"Hell yeah, I'm touching myself. What you think?"

"Stop doing that," I moaned with absolutely no resolve.

"You stop first," he whispered back.

Our moans were in sync, him stroking himself and me flicking my swollen nub with the tips of my fingers.

I was close when my moans grew loud in volume, echoing off my wooden walls.

"You were always so *fucking* loud," he reminisced in my ear. "Get yours, baby. Enjoy that on me."

My body shuddered, toes curled, eyes rolled as I held a fold in my sheets in the grip of my hand and I screamed my release.

"Yes, La *damn,*" he whispered through the phone's speaker. "You sound so beautiful."

A satisfied pulse coursed through my veins when I finally willed my body to relax, my chest rising and falling in my attempt to steady my breathing.

After about a minute of silence, I whispered, "I miss you," immediately regretting my admission.

That damn wine.

"I miss you more," Pryce replied.

My eyes became heavy when I reached for the phone and took it off speaker, pressing the device to my ear.

"Goodnight Pryce."

"WHAT!" he hollered. "Nah, nah, nah, La, wait, hold up—"

Before he could finish his thought, I ended the call and powered off my phone.

————

"So... I've been masturbating for the past week and my decision to do so made me do a very stupid and probably career ending thing."

I warmed the edge of the leather chaise in my therapist-friend's office in Brooklyn.

Liz sat across from me in one of the armchairs, her eyes damn near ready to pop out of her head. "Come again?"

"Oh I've been coming *a lot,* so what's one more time, right?"

She snorted a laugh and gave into a chuckle. I joined her.

"I'm sorry." She held up her hand apologetically. "Is this a regular therapy session or are we talking as friends again?"

"As friends, *please,* I beg." I pressed my palms together in a prayer-like fashion. "The last thing I need right now is for you to analyze me or the shit hole I've dropped myself in. I've beaten myself up enough already, beginning from when I ended my phone call with Pryce."

"Pryce?!" She tilted her head to one side. "Okay, did I miss something?"

"Yes, a lot, so let me catch you up." I moved to the edge of my seat. "I Googled him last Friday and happened upon a sex tape he filmed with some faceless woman. Watched a few minutes of it and thought it was only right to relieve myself because surprisingly that was the kind of effect the video had on me."

"Oh-kay...?"

"That was a few days before his session," I explained. "So now, yester-day, during his session, he goes into this spiel about all the things he wants to do to me and I let it get to my head."

"So you went home with those thoughts and masturbated?"

"And called him." I popped my lips. "We had phone sex, Liz. I had phone sex with an ex I thought I hated who might end up being a possible client and who has an alleged sex addiction."

"Oh my—" Liz covered her mouth then ran her fingers through her salt and pepper curls, giggling to herself. "Leelah, *what?*"

"See? Shit hole!" I pressed my hand to my forehead. "I don't know what got into me. I mean, I had wine, *a lot* of wine, too much damn wine. I couldn't get out of my head what he said to me. It's been two years since I've orgasmed and it seems I've been making up for lost time because one orgasm has not been enough. I just... I don't know, but I'm worried."

"Well," she began, "when you said you would practice sexual abstinence, we agreed it was the best thing to do since you were using sex as a coping mechanism and not in a way to connect with your partners. But you promised the moment you found someone you believed you could have a future with, you would end the vow with yourself to make a new vow with that new someone."

"Yes, *new* someone, not old. I didn't intend to move backwards. Pryce couldn't possibly be that *someone worth* doing all that for."

"And why not?"

"He broke my heart."

"Well, maybe he would be the right one to heal it?"

I stared at her. "Are you speaking to me as a friend or a therapist right now?"

"A little of both." She smiled, her eyes crinkling at the corners. "This thing that happened between you and Pryce while you were in high school was a time ago."

"Still registers as fresh to me every time I see him."

"Granted." Liz nodded. "And normally I'd say, no. He's now a possible client with a claim that he's addicted to sex. But... you think his claim is fictitious and you would know better than me."

I nodded.

"I'd also tell you the past is the past, leave it in your rear-view mirror, but there's something in him pulling you back in his direction. You called him to have phone sex. *You* called *him*. Your actions are ringing some alarms in my head."

I pinched the bridge of my nose.

"You're still attracted to him."

"I mean, you've seen him! The man is gorgeous, and he's only gotten better on the eyes with time."

"So," she continued, "his outer shell is appealing to you, always has been, but that isn't it, it doesn't stop there between you two. The physical attraction is one thing but the moment he stepped back into your life, you were reacting instantly with your heart, not your other body part. The mention of his name sends you into a tailspin. You've admitted to still being in love with him despite all the time that has passed. This isn't only a physical thing, Leelah and I think you agree. Physical would have been easier to get over if it were only that. Things may have started off physical with you two when you were younger and that may be what's fueling this thing between you now. But there's something within that physical that's forming a deeper connection between you two that you can't quite decipher and honestly, neither can I."

I twisted my lips to one side, mulling over her words.

"I've seen you discuss men who you were only physical with and I've seen you discuss Pryce and the two are like different seasons."

"So what are you suggesting I do?"

"Follow your heart," she replied. "You're extremely cerebral, sometimes to a fault. Very much in your head. In this situation, where Pryce has popped back up in your life, your mind and your heart are at war. Ironically, and as crazy as this might sound - your heart might be your guiding light."

"Debatable."

"I wouldn't expect you to say anything less. But humor me and ask yourself; what is your heart telling you to do?"

I parted my lips to speak, but she raised a finger to stop me.

"Don't answer the question *for* me. That part is all your business and none of mine, since this session is between friends." She smiled. "Sit with your reply and make your move based on that."

Twelve

"**E**veryone is dying to find out, are you staying with the *Flames* or starting the new season with the *Bronx Ballers*?"

I occupied a seat in a secluded corner at *Half & Half*, a bar and restaurant near the heart of the city. Beside me was Mykal Jones, a journalist for *For The Culture* magazine.

For The Culture was a monthly black entertainment publication co-owned by her cousin, singer and actor Amir Jones, and a friend of mine, Corey Barnes. Corey and I also owned a few rental basketball courts here in New York and on the west coast, so when I got the call to take part in an interview and to grace the cover, I was all in.

"You right about that," I replied. "My plans seem to be on everyone's mind."

My security guards, as usual, were only a walking distance away. On a Friday evening, the after-work crowd filled the restaurant and couldn't keep their eyes off me. This was the norm. Show up somewhere and unintentionally make others stop what they're doing to stare. Only a few approached to ask for an autograph or a picture, but most respected my space on the east coast.

"So?" Mykal asked, a smile beaming off her lips. "What are you going to do? The *Ballers* could use your help."

"They definitely can, for sure."

"But..." She grinned. "You have *'Property of La La land'* tatted on your left pec which I discovered in photos taken during your photo shoot for your editorial. New tat?"

"Got it at the start of the year."

She nodded. "Well, that new tattoo is making it abundantly clear Cali is home sweet home for you these days."

"Nah, my tat means more than you think." I ran my hand down my beard. "I'm still deciding on what to do to be honest, but the *Ballers'* fans have been treating me good out here, making it real hard not to want to stay."

"Well this *is* your hometown." She batted her eyelashes. "You were born in Brooklyn, correct?"

"Born and raised." I confirmed and smiled. "So yeah, it is my hometown. Playing for the *Ballers* before I retire would make everything come around full circle."

"Retirement?" Her brows arched. "Is that a serious consideration at this time?"

"Absolutely," I replied. "I'm interested in moving onto the next phase of my life, you know?"

"And what does the next phase entail?"

I snickered.

"Marriage, kids?" she probed.

"Both, hopefully."

"*Hmmm,*" she hummed, her eyes sparkling. "And do you have someone in mind for your future plans?"

A smile pulled at my lips.

"Off the record, of course," she added. "Present company is very interested in this scoop."

I twisted my head in her direction, and she winked at me.

"Oh really?"

She bit her bottom lip and bowed her head bashfully.

Mykal was a beautiful woman. In her late 20s, petite but curvy with a short haircut she liked to wear slicked back. A very professional woman about her business. Her skin was smooth and brown, and the color of raw cacao powder. She had the darkest eyes that sparkled like black diamonds. She was stunning, but she wasn't Leelah. I couldn't get Leelah off my mind if I tried. Especially after the other night.

"Are you single?" Mykal inquired.

"For now."

"For now? So someone *is* on your radar?"

"Still off the record?" I asked.

She licked her lips. "If you want it to be."

I scratched the back of my head.

"Hearts will break if it goes viral that Mr. Pryce Williams is suddenly ready to settle down with someone, you understand that, right?"

"Breaking hearts is the last thing I'd want to do."

She stared at me for a moment, a smile stretching her lips in either direction. "You are so damn handsome. I can't even take it."

I offered an impish smirk, pressing my hand to my chest, feigning offense. "Mighty forward of you, Ms. Mykal Jones."

"I'm just saying." She shrugged. "And you're aware of it, too."

"Well..."

She leaned forward to press the red button on her recorder, turning it off.

"Every time we sit down for an interview, I drop the hints and I know for a fact you notice them but you haven't yet taken the bait. What's up with that? How much more obvious do I have to be?"

My phone vibrating in my pocket pulled my focus off her. I retrieved the device and peeked down at the screen to see Leelah's name sprawled across it.

"Uh..." I hopped up and out of my seat immediately. "I gotta take this."

"Oh. Yeah. Of course." She nodded, leaning back in her seat and moving her eyes off me. "Go ahead, please."

I nodded back and turned to approach the bar, my security close behind.

"Dr. Waters," I answered.

"Mr. Williams," she replied, before giggling.

We were both silent for a moment after that.

"Am I interrupting something?" she asked.

"No, nah." I turned to glance over my shoulder to see Mykal packing up her things. "I was just finishing an interview for a magazine."

"Fancy," she purred into the phone. Her voice made me stiffen in my jeans a little. "So, I want to invite you to dinner. It's not as fancy as a magazine interview, but..."

I arched my brows.

"Dinner the other night didn't go over too well," she continued, "so I want to make up for that."

"Great," I said, my voice rising a few octaves. I cleared my throat and added, "I'm down. Where did you have in mind?"

"My place."

Blood rushed to my dick instantly, and I had to adjust the seat of my pants to accommodate the hard-on forming at the crotch.

"*Your* home? Word?"

She laughed, and I couldn't help but to snicker at her response.

"Yeah, *word*."

"Aight," I agreed. "I'm not about to be stupid and say no to an invitation from you."

Leelah giggled. "Tomorrow night at eight."

"Should I bring anything?"

"Just yourself."

I bit at my bottom lip. "Is this an invitation on a professional level or...?"

"Uh... more cordial, social. Really, just to talk and build a new rapport—" She stopped short of rambling. "Listen, Pryce, about the other night—"

"Please don't explain the other night," I insisted. "I *loved* what happened the other night. You tortured the shit out of me, but I deserved it. Plus, you were drinking..."

"Yeah, I know," she interjected. "But still, that was *so* not what I should've done. It was wrong on all accounts and I was in a crazy headspace—"

"Don't worry about it." I peeked over my shoulder to see Mykal still seated. "We can talk more about it tomorrow night at eight."

"Okay, yeah. That sounds good."

There was some silence again before she said, "Bye Pryce."

"Later, La."

I turned on my sneakers and made my way back to the area where Mykal sat, I presumed still waiting for me.

"I see the person on the other end of your phone put a little bounce in your step," she teased as I approached.

I lifted, then dropped my shoulders, remaining up on my feet.

"I just wanted to say goodbye," she said. "Your interview will appear in next month's publication. I think by then, you would have made your decision, probably would have announced it."

She scooted to the edge of her seat and stood up. "And the woman you were on the phone with is a lucky lady."

"How did you guess it was a woman?"

"Because I have a sixth sense about these things." She bit back her smile, glancing down at her taupe booties that showed a peek of her pink toenails. "She's lucky."

"I'm a luckier man."

Her jaw dropped. "Luckier man because you two are seeing each other? Can I get that on the record?! *Please* say on the record?"

I chuckled.

"Pryce Williams smitten." She gestured with her hand and used the space in front of her as if it were paper and her words the next headline. "I like this better than the story I originally had planned. I'd definitely get promoted to editor with this kind of scoop."

"Off the record for now, Mykal."

She dropped her head back between her shoulders. "You're breaking my heart, Pryce. Both professionally and emotionally."

"Aww, no, I'm sorry," I apologized with a pout.

Mykal stared at me for a moment before shaking her head.

"She's *so* lucky, *ugh*. And I kinda hate her for it."

I laughed.

"All right," she said, taking steps away. "Call me if you change your mind... on either thing."

I shook my head to myself, then focused down on my phone.

Dinner with Leelah... alone. She said it was dinner on a *"cordial, social"* vibe, making it the perfect opportunity to step my game all the way up and make my plans for us a reality.

Now I just have to figure out how to pull this shit off.

I took a seat and reached for my drink of gin and tonic, bringing the glass up to my lips.

"Here's to not fucking this up," I whispered before taking a sip.

THIRTEEN

LEELAH

One by one, I dropped four whole cloves of garlic into my sauce pan, watching as they sunk into the bubbling tomato cream sauce. Sade's voice echoed around my loft as she crooned the lyrics to "Ordinary Love." Her vocals were like soft kisses to the collarbone; smooth, unhurried, and gentle. She was such a vibe. The song was one of my favorites from her catalog. I'd been streaming her playlist from the moment I pulled out the first pot to cook. It was poignant, this song played on cue considering what was happening that night.

I was cooking for *Pryce*.

I snickered to myself at the thought while stirring the sauce.

If someone would have told me a month prior that I would prepare a meal for my ex who broke my heart years ago, I'd think they were high off something. Yet here I was, standing over a stove, dressed in a navy blue and white tie-dye knot front cami top and slit skirt that hugged my hips and teased the sight of my thigh.

I talked myself out of going through with the dinner at least twice that morning. I considered calling Pryce the day before and telling him to forget stopping by for dinner. The thing was, I'd already sent him my address and knew if I canceled with him, he would still show up. That was just his style.

I unscrewed the cap off my bottle of vodka and added at least half a cup to the sauce. Penne a la vodka was his favorite. I was making his favorite food.

"What the hell is wrong with me?" I asked out loud.

A heartbeat later, I angled the spout of the bottle in front of my lips and took a swig of the vodka to calm my nerves.

"Ordinary Love" continued humming in the background of my selfless act, the bass strings strumming as Sade's voice faded out. If Pryce and my situation had a soundtrack, this would be the first song played.

My eyes shifted to the large pot of salted water that rumbled with bubbles. I grabbed the bag of pasta, opened it, then poured it in.

A second later, I heard the buzz of my bell.

My breath hitched.

Instantly, my heart pounded. I stood frozen in my kitchen until my bell buzzed a second time. I grabbed the dishrag, turned the stove down on the sauce so it simmered as I made my way to my door.

More than likely, my doorman let Pryce up without informing me via phone call first. I imagine shock made him forget protocol the moment he saw a superstar basketball player push through the front door.

I sighed as I moved closer, then balanced myself on the arches of my feet. Peering through the fisheye lens peephole, I spotted someone behind Pryce, his hand holding onto the handle of a pushcart.

"What in the world?" I mumbled.

I unlocked the locks and pulled my door open.

Pryce stood on the other side smiling, in his hand at least two dozen stems of white calla lilies. I couldn't help but to return the smile. My eyes drifted past him and to the gentleman standing with his head high and shoulders back. He wore a smile on his face as he held onto a cart full of wines.

"Wow," I breathed. My eyes returned to Pryce when I asked. "What is all of this?"

Pryce's eyes were already working down my frame. His focus were my thighs when he asked, "Can we come in first?"

"Oh! Yeah." I stepped aside. "Come in, come in."

Pryce laid the calla lilies in my arms before proceeding past me, and I brought them to my nose to inhale. "*Mmm*, thank you."

"You're very welcome," he replied.

As Pryce's eyes roamed around what was visible from the front area of my loft, my eyes landed on the gentleman and the cart full of wine. He was much shorter than Pryce, appeared to be a little younger in age too, and he sported a beautiful *Kodak* grin.

"Hi," I said to him.

"Nice to meet you, Leelah," he greeted. "Pryce has been talking about you for years so I feel like I already know you."

I turned to find Pryce in front of my bookcase, examining the book spines in my collection.

"Oh has he?"

Pryce turned to face me, his smile seeming to never have left his lips. "La, this is Darnell. He's my assistant and has been for the past four years."

"It's very nice to meet you, too, Darnell," I told him. "And what's all of this?" I pointed at the cart full of bottles.

"I know how much you enjoy drinking wine," Pryce announced, pulling my attention back on him. The smirk he wore now made me ball my lips. I was very sure what he meant by me *enjoying* wine. "I wasn't sure which one you favored more so I got them all... well, at least what was available for me to get."

I tucked my lips into my mouth to keep from laughing. "That seems reasonable."

I moved closer to the cart and confirmed he indeed bought several wines. They all were either red, white, rose, dessert, or sparkling. Each falling under subcategories like dry white wine or fruity red. Even more detailed, like spicy or tannic. Each bottle sat in its own box with its own neatly handwritten label.

"My God," I gushed after I'd reviewed every bottle. They were all expensive, a few wines I've always wanted to try but couldn't convince myself to spend that kind of cash on a bottle. "Did you buy the whole wine store?"

"I did, actually," Pryce replied. "One bottle of each wine they had for sale."

My jaw dropped.

"I'll leave you two now," Darnell announced.

"Thanks, D," Pryce said before turning to continue his personal tour of my loft.

"It was nice meeting you," I told Darnell as he pulled open my loft's door, stepped out, and closed it.

I approached the door to lock it when Pryce said, "Your place is stunning, Dr. Waters."

I had no idea why him referring to me by my professional title had such an effect on me, but it did. That simple thing sent a rush of energy to the epicenter of my core and made my walls throb. It was a turn on. I gathered my breath at the door.

"Thank you," I replied, turning to make my way into my kitchen.

Testing the pasta in the pot, I noticed the penne was a little less al dente and drained it immediately.

"You have a real loft, loft," he continued. "Raw open space and barreled ceilings. It gets a little cold during the winter, doesn't it?"

"Like an ice box," I replied, adding the cooked pasta to the vodka sauce and lowering the fire again. "I have to increase the heat to keep the place at least at room temperature."

It didn't dawn on me that Pryce entered the kitchen area until I felt him exhale inches behind me. "I know the chill is especially diffi-cult to tolerate when you don't have someone here to keep you warm."

Instinctively, I turned to face him and noticed the devilish grin on his face.

"Who told *you* that?"

He swiped the tip of his tongue backward and against his molars. "Touché."

I fought my smile and twisted to face the pot again. "The food is almost ready."

"I hope you know I'm not hungry for that," he informed.

"Why not?" I glanced at him over my shoulder. "It's penne a la vodka."

"Yup, my favorite, and it means so much to me that you remembered that."

"So you don't want it?" I spun around to face him now, to find him licking his lips. "This is the only thing on the menu, so if you don't want it..."

"I want it. I also have an appetite for something that can't be made on a stove."

The spark in his eyes when he said that was impossible to miss. I rolled my eyes at it.

"When I invited you for dinner, I invited you for *dinner*. That's it."

"Is it?"

I took a breath to calm the pounding of my heart, then pointed at a chair at my glass kitchen table. "Sit down, Pryce."

He threw his hands up, palms facing me. "Yes ma'am... Dr. Waters."

I turned quick to hide my smile. If I could be honest, sleeping with Pryce crossed my mind even before I extended the invitation for him to join me for dinner at my place. But I'd shot the possibility down the moment I considered it. Honestly, I just wanted to talk, feel him out without any distractions.

Or did I?

Everything was becoming more and more unclear as my body heated up from just being in the same room with him again.

I plated the food and grabbed a bottle of *Sangiovese* off the pushcart. This wine was bright and fruity. I remembered it from one of the tastings I attended with a group of friends a year prior. I recalled it going well with creamy sauces, so I knew it would compliment the meal.

A few minutes later, I took my seat across from Pryce, forking pasta into my mouth then taking slow swigs of wine, watching him do the same over the rim of my glass.

Tonight, he showed up dressed more formal. Tailored black slacks, matching black shirt with a hem that hung over his waistline, stopping just a few inches past his columnar thighs. On his feet were these sexy butterscotch-tinted loafers.

The shirt wasn't baggy nor was it fitted, but it did a bad job of concealing his fit form. Staring at him made me gulp my wine faster than I should have.

Keep it social, cordial, Leelah. Social cordial...

"So," I started, "how's your father?"

He wrinkled his brows. "Good, I guess. I only hear from him when he needs a little cash, which honestly I can't complain about that. The less contact I have with Gregory Williams, the better."

Pryce's relationship with his dad was always never the best. From the time I've known Pryce, he and his dad spent a crazy amount of time apart, more than I felt was normal. His dad worked a lot, giving Pryce a lot of time alone. He practically raised himself. The strain Pryce's mother left when she abandoned the both of them when Pryce was young had never really been worked out. Because the night was not about that, I chose not to push Pryce to unpack. Discussing his mother could have easily morphed into a nightlong therapy session with revelations that would only scratch the surface.

Pryce picked up the bottle of wine and refilled my glass, keeping his eyes on me.

"You seem eager to refill my glass."

His tongue licked at his lips, licking the sauce from it. "I like you on wine. I like it a lot."

I giggled, and he flashed a smile.

"But seriously, this meal is delicious La," he complimented.

"Thank you." I smiled. "It's been a while since I've made it."

"I like that you thought of me when you did."

I lifted my glass to my lips and sipped slow.

"How many other men have you cooked for?" he inquired, eyes down on his plate as he forked more pasta.

"Not enough," I answered, focusing my attention on my plate as well. "To be honest, my dates and I never really got to eat much together since other things took priority. You know?"

I looked up from my plate to see him chewing hard, jaw bone protruding with each bite. I had to force myself to swallow back a laugh.

"Bet you wish you didn't ask that, huh?" I poked.

"Hmph," he huffed, stabbing his fork into another pile of pasta. "Social cordial 'bout to raise my damn blood pressure."

My giggle turned into a laugh, and Pryce cracked a smile in response.

Once we cleared our plates, I stood to grab my dish and his.

He stood too. "I'll help you out."

"Pryce Williams clearing his area?" I teased while approaching my kitchen's counter. "I know for a fact you do not do that often."

"I'm rarely around my first love."

I blinked in response.

"So, for that reason," he continued, placing the dishes down in my sink, "I gotta do shit like this to impress her."

I laughed.

He closed the space between us and I stepped back, not able to go too far with my kitchen counter stopping my escape.

"I know I've said it several times already, but your laugh is still so sexy," he whispered.

I exhaled all the air I had in me through my mouth. My nipples hardened behind my crop top and I was slowly losing the strength to remain on my feet.

"Pryce," I whispered.

"Let's stop all this cordial shit and get real, aight?"

I folded my lips in my mouth and bit down.

"Where did you masturbate that night you called me?"

He stood inches away from me now. Pryce kept his hands to himself, but with his eyes he touched me all over. His scent was enchanting. Amber and sandalwood commingling with his natural aroma. He oiled his skin so well, the man smelled edible.

"We can't," I declared, quickly realizing where this between us was heading.

"I didn't sleep after that night you called me, you know that right?" he revealed. "I finished myself off as best I could. Made quite a mess of myself, too, in the process. But I couldn't rest after hearing you moan in my ear again. After all this time, that moan of yours ignites something in me that leaves me feeling like a feign for you. So I spent the night Googling your name, hoping for your address to pop up so I could show up here and relive you and myself the proper way."

I traced the contours of his face with my eyes, falling even deeper into his trance.

"If I haven't made this clear to you yet, La, allow me to make it real obvious now - I. Want. You. Not only physically but we can definitely get physical tonight with your permission of course."

He laid his hands against my hips, and it took everything in me to remain on my feet. Pryce slid those multi-million dollar hands up slowly, mapping the curve of my hips with his fingertips, smoothing up my waist and stopping at the globe of my breasts.

I tossed my head back, trying my best to remember to breathe, wanting to be disciplined enough to push him off, but knowing that would not happen. Not tonight, and not after getting this close again. I feared the feeling he provided, the zing to my core, would go away if I did.

Why does such a bad idea feel so damn good?

He cupped my breasts in his hands, running his thumbs over my erect nipples, now visible through my top.

I glanced up to find his bottom lip tucked in his mouth, his lids low over his pupils. He stared at me through the slits of his eyes, a stare I never had the power to resist.

"Pryce..."

"The only words I want to hear from you after my name is where your room is and how fast or slow you want me to pace my strokes."

I cocked a brow, and he challenged me by cocking his too.

"You're well aware I'm abstaining from sex," I reminded. "And as we discussed, you'll have to, too—"

"Can we not tonight, though?" Pryce leaned in close, pressing his body to mine. He bent his long legs at the knees to align his mouth with the maze of my ear when he asked, "Can you be a little bad with me, La? Can we bend your rule tonight? 'Cause I have plans to reintroduce myself to you. Body to body." He sucked the lobe of my ear into his warm mouth, and my knees buckled. Pryce caught the weight of me in his hands and held me up against the counter.

"Or do you want me to stop?" he whispered next.

Damn this man.

"If you want me to stop..." He gripped my jaw with his free hand to level my lips with his mouth. "... you can tell me to stop and I'll pause everything, without question."

It was like it happened in slow motion. The lowering of his breath to mine and that initial brush of his lips. A moan escaped from me, and he moaned in response.

And *that* was my undoing.

"No," I panted in his mouth. "Don't stop."

Pryce crushed his lips against mine, and I exhaled a breath I didn't realize I'd been holding.

I parted my lips to welcome his tongue. Reactively, he groaned. And the moment our tongues reunited after years of being apart, those metaphorical sparks flew.

Smacking noises sounded around us next. I lost myself on him, totally drifting into his world again. All the hesitation I had in me, all the talking I did with myself that morning regarding not doing anything besides having dinner with him, slowly fell to the wayside.

I should've known better. Should've known being in a room with Pryce, alone, was a setup for moral failure. A failure my body was interpreting as a win.

Pryce broke our kiss with ease and stepped back to grab the hem of his shirt, pulling it up and over his head before removing it. He turned briefly to toss his top on the chair he occupied earlier, then returned to his stance in front of me.

I tilted my head to the side when I recognized it, his tattoo.

I lifted my hand to the words written in black without even thinking. I pressed my fingertips to the writing and outlined the words etched on his left pec. A tattoo that mimicked branding often seen on cattle. A huge smile pulled at my lips before I crawled my eyes up to meet his.

"You did *not* tattoo this on you!" I cupped my hand over my mouth to hide my smile, remembering when I'd first heard him say it.

"Can I come through?" he asked.

It rained that night, poured. Weathermen issued a flash flood warning, but that didn't stop Pryce from driving to my house and sitting outside at the curb. It was the last few days of December. My father was away making his final rounds of the year before he was off until the new year. He had plans to return the next night. Exhaustion kept my sister Gena knocked out. Finals had taken a lot out of her, and she'd been catching up on sleep.

"It's late, Pryce," I whispered into the phone, grabbing a pillow to wedge between my thighs.

"But I need to get into La La Land tonight."

I giggled low. "La La Land? Where the hell is that?"

"Mmm, that pussy."

I laughed, louder this time.

"Greatest place on earth," he explained. I could tell he was smiling and licking his lips even through the phone. Pryce always did that when he talked about what laid between my thighs. "The only place I feel at home, baby," he added. "It's my sanctuary."

"Oh, your sanctuary, huh? Using big SAT words on me now?"

He chuckled. "Just speaking from the heart, baby... and my dick."

I howled a laugh. "Aww, Pryce, you are so sweet and so nasty at the same time."

He moaned. "I'd love to get real nasty with you. Are you gonna let me in so I can do that?"

"I sure did." He smiled. His hands moved down there, sliding his palm past my skirt's slit. He only stopped when his fingers laid at the seat of my panties. "The only home I acknowledge."

"*Property of La La Land* though?" I questioned.

"You see where it is? Right on my heart." His smile slid off his face, and he gazed at me with serious eyes. "You own me."

My brows wrinkled over watering eyes. I tried my best to blink back the tears.

"To me? I'm yours forever until the day I take my last breath." He nodded. "I belong to you in every which way. Ain't nothing changed."

"Pryce," I said with more breath than tone. But before I could say another word, he pressed his lips to mine again and kissed me with everything he had in him.

So wrapped up in the moment and because I'm such a sucker for that man... I fell under his spell again.

I allowed him to lift me off my feet and to pull my legs around his waist to carry me up to my room. I guess he figured out where it was on his own because before I knew it, we were there.

He gently laid me on the bed. His hands reached for the band of my slit skirt and pulled it down. I lifted enough to help with the removal. Next his hands were at the crop top, slipping it off me.

I laid there before him in only my bra and panties, him in front of me only dressed in his pants. Pryce grabbed me by the legs and guided me to the foot of the bed, closer to him. Down in front of me, he peeled my panties off and placed his thumb to the top of my pussy. He leaned forward and pressed his lips to my lower lips. I gasped and almost unraveled with him doing only that.

"She's still as pretty as I remember." He parted my lips with his, his tongue swiping up the length of my slit slow.

My back arched off the bed, and my voice bounced off the walls. Soon he buried his face between those lips. Licking, sucking, blowing, then flicking. He dipped his tongue inside of me and lapped at my essence. My hand was on the crown of his head as he moved his mouth from side to side, tonguing an orgasm so intense out of me, I saw stars when I closed my eyes.

This was not the plan when I invited him here. Or was it?

It didn't matter in that moment, anyway. Nothing else did, in fact. Not that he may have had a sex addiction. Not that he'd broken my heart. Not that he was Pryce Williams, *NBA* superstar.

No. He was just Pryce. My first boyfriend, first kiss, first love, and the first man to break my heart. He was my first everything. And if tonight was all we had, I would acknowledge its worth.

Pryce pushed his hand into his slacks pocket and pulled out a handful of condoms, dropping them onto the bed.

"We'll sleep in the morning, aight?" he promised.

I had no time to respond because within moments he'd crawled on top of me, his lips back on mine.

I tasted myself on his tongue, pressed my hands to his cheeks to prolong our lip-lock. He undid the button on his slacks and pulled them off with my help, me pushing his boxers off too with the heel of my foot. He balanced himself on his knees for only a moment to rid himself of the rest of his clothes, and that was enough time for me to rise up and off my back to wrap my mouth around the length of him.

"*Gahdamn,*" he groaned.

For the first few minutes he relinquished control, only combing his fingers through my curls while holding me by the back of my head. Each time I locked my jaw around his erection, he dropped his head back between his shoulders and his hips jerked forward.

"La, where you learned to—oh my God! Damn, woman." He tried to pull from my hold. "I'm about to come, baby, hold on one second." I tightened my grip and held him by the hips, never pausing my bobbing, feeling his heavy rod spasming between the bed of my tongue and the roof of my mouth. He exhaled a moan once the first spurt hit the back of my mouth, then strained a groan when he let himself go completely down my throat.

"The fuck?!" Pryce breathed, chest heaving in the air once I finally released him. "When the hell you started doing that? Damn!" He stumbled back. "You tryna take my fucking soul?!"

I licked my lips of him, shrugged, and drawled out, "I mean..."

He cocked his head to the side. Shock was quickly replaced with that devilish grin from earlier.

"Come here," he growled, grabbing me by the ankles. I squealed when he pulled me closer and positioned me beneath him.

Pryce ran the head of his sheathed erection up and down the most sensitive part of me. I breathed in and out of my mouth, willing myself not to pass out from anticipation. And when he finally pushed himself in, my inhale mimicked his entrance.

I was tight, damn near unyielding, and Pryce realized this with his first attempt to go deeper. Much like my first time with him, he pressed his lips to mine and slid his tongue into my mouth. Rolled his hips back and forth with a little more gusto.

"Open up for me, baby," he whispered on my lips.

He delivered smooth, concise pumps. Each time he rolled his hips back and pushed forward, he stroked another inch in until he finally buried his bone completely.

My jaw hung open the whole time he filled me to the hilt. I dug my nails into his back in response.

Pryce didn't stop filling me until the trimmed grains of hairs on his pelvis grazed my clit.

"Good girl," he whispered. "You've never run from it."

His pelvis pulled back, then met mine again as he pumped in and out, repeating the action in an almost choreographed routine. Pryce anchored me in the moment, giving me no opportunity to think of anything or being anywhere else connected to him.

I was loud, so loud, my moans echoed around us. Painting the walls with audio and the wooden barrel ceiling, too. There was no way no one heard me that night.

"*Mmm*, she remembers me." He groaned as he sped up his pace.

I shut my eyes and angled my hips so he'd continue hitting that spot that sent me everywhere but here.

He interlocked his fingers with mine. "Was this what you were on the hunt for, La?"

I couldn't answer, couldn't think. All I was capable of doing in that moment was feeling. Feeling the stretch of my walls as I accommodated his girth. The slip and slide of his hard-on as he wound his hips and drove into me in sync with his exhales.

Pryce rocked into me with precision, his hips angled with mine. So each time he dipped low, I felt him in the spot that mattered the most.

"You'll never find it elsewhere, love." He groaned when it got too good. "You'll always come up short on that search."

I gasped at the friction building and pressed the back of my head into the pillow.

"Because this thing right here, that's making you shake below me..." He hung his head forward between his shoulders and sucked in air through his teeth. "This thing that's got me weak right now for you... it ain't a sex thing, it's an *us* thing and no one can play substitute to that."

He grabbed me by the waist and we turned over, me taking my place on top. I found my pace quick, oscillating my hips against him, my ass sliding back and forth over his lap. A tingling sensation ran through me, starting from the root of my hair and bottoming out at the tip of my toes. Quick breaths were the only option to keep air flowing in and out of me, but even that was a luxury.

He balanced himself on his elbows, his eyes locked on mine before they moved to my hips. He watched me work, his jaw slacked, eyes struggling to stay open. Soon he freed one hand to grip my ass, then dropped his head back between his shoulders and grunted each time I rode his dick into me.

"The student has become the teacher on me," he panted. Pryce pushed up and turned me over to my stomach, using only my legs.

His hands were at my waist when he pulled me into position and slid into me again. Pryce always took forever to come and so did I, which made for a fun race to see who could get to their finish line first. I always beat him to it though, and this time was no different.

He slammed into me from the back. Gathered my hair in one hand and held a fist full of my curls in his grip while he slapped my ass with the other, causing me to miss a breath.

Soon my body heated, and my legs trembled.

"Yes," I moaned, grateful to be reunited with a cresting sensation I'd been missing for years.

He exhaled behind me, his arm curving my waist, fingertip connecting with my clit. "Let me make it last for you."

I pushed back against him until the orgasm that had been building up rippled through me in waves. Pryce increased his pace, deepened his stroke, now circling my pink pearl with even more accuracy. I had the folds of my sheets in my grip, trying my hardest to tether myself to the bed. A weightless feeling sent my eyes rolling as I released silent cries.

"*Mm-hmm* La," he whispered behind me. "Take your time with it, baby."

It was like being body-snatched, no longer in control, vulnerable and raw, just open to everything. His breaths grew heavy behind me. My voice returned and my walls fluttered around his erection. Seeing anything was impossible because my eyes kept rolling to the back of my head.

The moment we'd reached the peak of our releases, and at the same time, a chorus of our moans and groans elevated to heights my loft's walls had never heard before.

"God, I love you," he strained before roaring his release around the surrounding space.

We fell out and onto the sheets when we'd had enough. Between my thighs throbbed with a sweet ache I've been craving for years.

The last thing I remembered was Pryce pulling me close to his chest, showering my neck with kisses and whispering he loved me into my shoulder blade as I fell asleep in his arms.

FOURTEEN

The next morning, I woke before her. My eyes blinked repeatedly in an effort to recall where I was. I twisted my head in her direction to find her still sound asleep. She was so beautiful, her wild curly hair lying in her face. Without giving it a second thought, I peeled back the sheets and slid down to between her warm thighs. Spread her legs gently, then buried my lips in the middle of her lower lips. I flitted my tongue over her clit gently, repeating the action until she started to stir in her sleep. A few flicks later, Leelah soon awoke to my tongue sweeping along her tiny ball. I covered her with wet warmth, greeting her as her eyes shot open and a moan escaped her without restraint.

Last night was the life I'd been waiting to get back to. The squeeze of her walls around me again, holding me tight like it never wanted to let me go to begin with. That was all I needed to understand exactly what I wanted with her. What I needed.

She peeled back the sheets to find me between her thighs, my tongue tracing the circumference of her clit.

I'd been craving her taste for years. A taste I foolishly searched for in the women I entertained. But no one could cure that hunger, and nothing made that more clear to me as I helped myself to breakfast in bed.

She closed her eyes again and pressed her hand to my head, rolling her hips in time with my tongue thrusts. Her moans grew louder and mine did too. I noticed a familiar arch in her back and the slight tremor in her leg, hinting her release was close. So I drew the ball of her clit into my mouth, kept the hood peeled back so I could wiggle my tongue at the crown of her sweet spot. I slid my tongue from left to right, never losing momentum, refusing to focus elsewhere except on the tip. I maintained my speed. That La La Land got off on consistency, and after all these years, nothing had changed. I didn't let up off it, watching as her orgasm hit her like a high-tide wave.

Her back arched even higher, her head rising up and off her pillow like she was possessed. Stuttered, raspy moans vibrated from her vocal chords. I balanced the nook of her knees over my shoulders and held on to her hips to keep her in place. I moaned against her pussy, indulging in the pulsing reaction against my lips.

When she met her end, her back slammed down against her mattress, and I joined her on my pillow.

"Damn," she whispered.

"Good morning to you too." I licked the rest of her off my lips.

Her breasts rose and fell with each breath she took, exposed, and calling me.

She twisted her head in my direction and giggled. "You're spoiling me."

"Nothing you don't deserve." I moved in closer and buried my lips in her neck. "Plus, I can't get enough of being in La La Land. You know that."

She laughed.

"I love you, La," I professed. "So fucking much."

The second I said those words, I felt the weight lift off me. I'd been wanting to tell her that since the first day I strolled into her office, because I did... love her. A lot.

She sighed. "Pryce."

"I need you back in my life."

She turned to face me.

"I understand this is a lot," I offered, staring at her. "And I'll admit this all seems so sudden. But you're my world. You've been my world, even though we've been over 3,000 miles apart these past few years."

Her eyes remained on me. I noticed the battle in her eyes. The fight happening inside of her and I just wanted to take it all away.

I told her, "Be with me."

"*Wow*," she exhaled. "I haven't even had coffee yet to ground me for this conversation."

I chuckled. "I couldn't wait any longer to tell you. Last night was great, I wouldn't trade it for a single moment and not for anything else in the world, but I want more than last night with you, La. I don't want last night to be *our* last night or our last time."

I was saying a lot, but I didn't have much time. We were four days into August. I needed to train for the new season, but more important than all that, I needed to confirm for myself which city I would call home - New York or Oakland.

"Pryce, you're asking for *too* much right now."

She peeled away from me to press her back to her leather headboard. "All I can give right now *is* last night."

My heart sank. "La, *please* don't tell me that."

"I'm being honest." Leelah ran her hand down her face. "What happened last night, and even this morning, shouldn't have occurred."

I dropped my head back against my pillow.

"And I'm not saying I regret it," she clarified. "I don't regret it in the least. But you're supposed to be my client. My client who claimed to have a sex addiction."

That damn Marc.

I grunted and shook my head.

"What we did goes against everything I stand for; what I've learned, my ethics, my vow to myself." She dropped her head into her hands, then ran her hands up and over her bed hair. "But there's just something about you I'm still tethered to, something I shouldn't still be attached to—"

"Is it that I cheated?" I asked. "Look, what I did was stupid. I was young." What I was about to tell her could either help me or sabotage this whole plan of getting her back, but I couldn't think of any other way to fix this. So I went for it.

I scraped my hand down my beard. "I was exposed to shit at a young age I shouldn't have seen yet. Renee opened my eyes so wide sexually that when you and I met, all I had to give was my heart because my heart was all you wanted. And I did give you my heart, something I never did with anyone before you. In return you gave me your body a decision I cherish to this day, I swear." I emphasized that by sliding my fingers up her thigh. "I didn't cheat on you in college because I had feelings for that girl. I did it because my young dumb ass believed I needed someone experienced just for one night. Someone who knew what to do without me telling them how to do it. It was stupid. *I* was stupid."

I had her attention.

"The shit I did with her, I would've never done with you at the time. You were so innocent to me back in the day, La. So pure and perfect. We were intimate, yes, but I had a whole Madonna-whore complex thing happening with you and didn't even realize it. But I'm grown now. It's clear now I can have both the angel and the vixen in you, and more. But the sex is not all I want though, baby. I want a soul tie with you. I want the whole package. The good, the bad, the sexy, the flaws. I want all that. I *need* all that—"

"Pryce." She raised a hand to stop me. "It's not just the cheating. It's your status now, too, that makes me uneasy about you possibly hurting me again."

My brows furrowed. "My status?"

"Yeah, your celebrity. Women throw themselves at you even more now." She turned her body to face me and I sat up too. "My secretary practically comes on herself when you step into a room, or just if your name is mentioned, and the girl works for me."

"La—"

Leelah pressed her fingers to my lips to stop me from speaking. "Even if we were to give this another shot, I would worry about you being unfaithful again. You had pussy thrown at you while you were in college and I thought that was a lot, but now... you're a fucking *NBA* superstar. You have women plotting on how to get even a moment alone with you and will go to lengths to do so whether or not you have a girlfriend."

"I don't give a fuck about them," I admitted, my nostrils flaring. "I don't give a shit about any of this! But I give a fuck about you. You can trust me—"

"No." She shook her head. "That's my point... I *can't*. At all. Hence the problem."

Her words sliced through me like a bag of blades right in my gut. I dropped my back against her headboard, my shoulders sagging in defeat. Trust was the hardest thing to get, but the easiest thing to lose. If she didn't trust me, that shit was damn near impossible to get back.

"You wanted Courtney because you believed she was more experienced and you got bored teaching me."

"I didn't say all that."

"You didn't have to," she voiced low. "I know what you meant when you said it."

We were quiet for a moment.

"Who's to say, there won't be a similar occurrence? Not necessarily the same situation, but a scenario where a woman will give you something I can't?"

"I'm off that shit, believe me. I'm about to retire," I declared. "I'm more than ready to leave the league and settle down."

She stared at me with her watering gray eyes.

"I want a family, La." I took her hand. "A wife and some kids, at least two. I want a house far from all this Hollywood-type shit. On a hill somewhere with a gang of land, no neighbors for miles. I want *you*, Leelah. Every time I picture the life I wish to have after all this, I consistently see your face."

"Pryce, I—"

"Please La, just at least think about it."

"There's no need for me to think about it though." Her bottom lip trembled. "My mind is made up. I'm sorry."

I cringed at the finality in her tone, then blew the hurt out through my mouth. I leaned close to her, pressed my lips to her cheek and left a kiss. "I'm gonna head out. Got a lot to take care of today."

That was a lie. It was Sunday, my off day. Usually I spent my off days indoors reading and chilling, but I had to get out of there.

Tears rimmed my lids as I pulled on my boxers and then my slacks.

"Pryce—"

"Just... think about it for me," I pleaded, turning to face her.

She parted her lips to speak, and I stopped her by raising a finger.

"All I want for you to do is to think about it, La. That's all I'm asking you to do right now. Give me at least that, *please*."

She puffed her cheeks with air and looked away, offering a reluctant nod.

With that, I made my way out of her room and down her stairs to grab my shirt to leave her loft. My heart hung in limbo, but still with hope she'd answer my plea favorably. I hoped she'd inevitably change her mind, but I also feared she really meant what she said about her mind already being made up.

FIFTEEN

Leelah

I rolled my chair closer to my desk. My legs bounced below the table once I found what little comfort I could find in my seat. The hour was later than usual, a little after 4 p.m., but I had one final client for the day - Pryce.

He warmed the seat across from mine, his eyes focused on me. Pryce padded into the office literally two minutes ago. The moment my secretary April announced his arrival, my heart took a nosedive into my stomach.

Now a Wednesday, Pryce and I hadn't spoken to each other after the Saturday night and Sunday morning we spent together. Nerves struck me every time I picked up the phone to call him. I feared him mentioning the prospect of *us* again.

"Okay." I placed my pen down on the desk. "So, how are you today?"

The session was his first official one with me. I'd decided the night after our hookup to go along with the foolery, even though I knew—"

"I don't have a sex addiction, La," he blurted.

That. I already knew *that,* and yet again my gut was right.

But I still asked, "And why do you feel you don't have a sex addiction? Isn't your addiction claim why you showed up here seeking my help?"

"I love you," he avowed in an easy tone. "I'm still in love with you."

I shut my eyes and held them tight together.

"And the other night only proved to me you still love me too."

I dropped my head, guiding my fingers up the bridge of my nose to pinch. "So, you lied?"

"Marc lied."

"And you main*tained* the lie."

He shrugged. "The lie was the only way I could see you."

I shook my head.

"You weren't going to meet with me any other way."

"This is why I can't trust you, Pryce. *This.*"

He squeezed his eyelids shut and punched the arm of the chair with a closed fist.

"La," he began, "we gotta make this right between us. I'm not addicted to sex but, baby, I'm addicted to us, to the future I've envisioned for us."

"Pryce, please—"

"Nah, you please." He scooted to the edge of his seat. "*Please* take me back. What happened, what I did to you... happened years ago. I'm not the same person. I'm a man now, Leelah."

"You and your friend devised a plan to get your ass in here and in my chair and you want to tell me you are not the same person?"

"I did that because I really want you back and would do anything to have you."

I opened up my desk drawer and threw my notepad inside. "I have real clients who tried to book an appointment today, Pryce. Real clients with real problems and you're in here wasting my time with this bullshit which I knew was bullshit but ignored my gut and went along with the bullshit and I shouldn't have. I knew better."

"And why'd you do that?"

"What?" I asked, my eyes ballooning. "Are you really going to ask me this question?"

"Yes, I'm really gonna ask you this question. Because I don't need help finding the answer, shorty."

"*Dr.* Waters," I corrected through my teeth.

"Dr. *Williams*, actually," he spat back. "If you'd stop being so difficult and allow this to happen between us."

I took a breath through my slacked jaw and pressed my back to my chair.

"I'm not trying to earn my way back with you to waste your time at work or in life. I want everything with you, Leelah, and I want all that shit now. I've always wanted a future with you."

I said nothing. My mind paused thinking the moment he alluded to wanting marriage with me. Granted, this was a discussion he brought up at my place Sunday morning when he pleaded his case similar to how he did in my office, but he was never this direct. *Never.* Not when we were dating all those years ago either.

"I want to marry you," he told me. "I want you to be my wife. The forever people talk about when they think of love? I want that forever with you. I *need* forever with you. So..." He stood from his seat and approached my desk, leaned over the surface and closer to me. "Tell me what I gotta do to earn my way back here..." He placed his big hand over my heart. "... and I promise, I swear on my life, it'll be done."

My eyes welled. The moment I blinked, tears trickled from them and lined my cheeks.

Pryce rounded my work desk and stopped in front of me. He crouched down and took my hand, using the other hand to swipe his thumb beneath my eyes.

"I hurt you," he admitted. "And I hate myself for hurting you. But I promise you I will never hurt you again. You're the one for me, La, the only one who has my heart. I've been with a lot of women..."

I scoffed and rolled my eyes.

"... and you've been with a lot of men," he continued. "Learning that shit cut me deep, I won't lie to you, but I get it. I understand why we gave that level of access to us, to those people. Why, after so many attempts with them, we kept on looking and sharing ourselves with strangers who were less deserving. We were looking for each other. You said you were searching for that thing? I was searching too. Everywhere. And like I told you, we will never find us outside of us, because that thing *is* us, beautiful. Exclusive to only you and me."

With every word he spoke, he spoke them from the heart and into mine, drawing me closer to him. His eyes were so sincere, clearly a hint he wasn't talking shit. This was the realist and rawest I'd ever seen him... but there was no way I was going to heel. Who told him he could do this? Break my heart, disappear, and return, pretty much telling me he's ready to be the man he should've been to me from the start? Fine, we were young, but was he too young to at least not break my trust in him back then? So what if *he's* ready? Does that mean *I* have to be too? Because, truthfully...

"Pryce," I whispered. I drew in a deep breath and with much needed courage told him, "I'm not ready to return to that place with you."

He fell back into a seat on the floor.

"We are different people now, that's true. But I can only weigh the truth of your promise based on past actions, and the past makes me uncomfortable. The past really hurt me."

"La..."

"Then now, in my present, you maintained a lie, yes to meet with me, but you let the lie go on for this long?"

"I've told you everything. I've owned up to fucking up, took full responsibility because the shit was my fault. It *was*." He brought his hands to his face and pressed his fingers to his lids. "I don't know what else you want from me."

"Nothing," I whispered. "Absolutely nothing and that's *exactly* my point."

He stared up at me.

"I gave you everything back then, Pryce. *Everything*, and way too soon. We were really young, I get that, but I envisioned my future with you when I looked at you even back then. As crazy as this might sound, I viewed you as my husband when we were only teenagers. I made plans around you. Everyone was talking about you being scouted and you definitely playing for the *NBA*, so I made an effort to prepare myself mentally for that. I gave you one of the most precious parts of me because I believed you were *it* for me." I shook my head. "So, when you slept with that girl, after she told me you would, despite your love for me, your decision to do so broke me. I never thought you had it in you. I thought for sure that yes, she could try, but my Pryce would never fall for her. He wouldn't hurt me like that... not *me*."

He exhaled, dropping his head forward.

"I can't change the past Leelah, I'm sorry," he admitted to the floor. Pryce looked up at me and shrugged. "All I can do is acknowledge my wrong, right my misstep, and progress forward, but if you're telling me changing as a person isn't enough for you, then..." Pryce balanced himself on his hands to stand up. "Then you're telling me there's nothing else I can do. And if that's how things are between us, then that's how things have to be."

I stared up at him, sniffing back my tears.

"I gotta go."

I pointed at the hourglass's bulb, still full of sand. "You still have time in your session."

"Bill me however much the session costs and a cancellation fee if you must, I don't care, Leelah. At this point, I don't care about anything else."

He turned to my door and twisted the knob, stepping out and closing the door behind him.

I remained in the same spot for a moment. My body stilled by his admission and finally his exit.

Sixteen

"**S**o what's going on, Pryce?" my boy, August, asked over the phone. "You need me to stop by in the morning to hook something up for you?"

"Well, of course." I rolled over onto my back in bed. "Let's aim for 11:30. Make it a brunch thing. Give me a chance to eat something healthy since I've been eating like trash every night."

August chuckled.

"Well, that's not entirely true." I smiled to myself, but that smile fell immediately. "Leelah made a little something that was better than anything else I've eaten out here."

August Hall was my boy from high school. A good friend who was also a chef, an alkaline vegan chef. He's been in magazines, on daytime talk shows, teaching the world how to nourish their minds, bodies, and souls through clean eating.

"Wait, what?!" he asked. "You've been seeing Leelah since you've been back home?"

I pushed air out of my mouth and into the phone. "I've been focused on doing more than that, but shorty is making it real hard for me to do it."

"*Wow*," he whispered.

"Yeah."

August knew Leelah pretty well. His late wife used to be friends with her in high school.

"How's Genesis?" I asked, trying to change the conversation. "How's wedding planning going?"

"Easy," he answered. From the effortless glide of his words, I could tell he was smiling. "We're planning a destination wedding. She insisted."

"That's exactly what I would do." I voiced. "Leave the church weddings to the traditionalists. I like it."

"Yup," he replied. "I cannot wait to make that woman my wife, man."

I couldn't blame him. Since he and Genesis started dating and got engaged two months after making things official, their relationship has been enviable to everyone who knew them. They were the perfect match.

"Yo..." I cleared my throat. "Let me ask you something."

"Shoot."

"Was it just as easy moving on?" I quizzed. "After Jasmine? Y'all were high school sweethearts. That's a relationship that seems impossible to get over."

"Jazmine and my relationship was really on the outs for years before her death, so to say our relationship was hard to get over would be a lie," he replied. "When you've loved someone for so long the way I love Genesis, you fall easy and you fall hard. And you do everything in your power to make it work, you know? You accept the difficult times that you know you'll get over because the love is that real and will get you through it. You understand?"

"I think I'm gonna have to move on from Leelah, man."

August made a clicking sound with his mouth. "It's like that?"

"It's like that."

"Hmph."

I bit my bottom lip and released it. "I'm headed back to Oakland on Sunday. Gonna negotiate a deal and sign with the *Flames* for two years, then probably retire the jersey."

"Damn." August exhaled into the phone. "Was kind of hoping to have my boy back on the east and not only have him popping in-and-out of town at will."

"Yeah, me too."

We were silent for a moment.

"Anyway." I sat upright in bed to swing my legs off it. "I'm about to head out, get into some shit tonight."

"What type of *shit*, P?"

I sighed. "Something other than sitting in this dark ass loft alone in my feelings, bruh."

"Don't do something you'll regret in the morning."

"Where the fuck is that coming from?" I asked, laughing.

"I'm just saying." He chuckled. "You're not sounding like the Pryce I know. If things concerning Leelah are weighing that heavy on your heart, sit with those feelings, my man. Sort through them. Then figure something out from there. But don't go out there trying to drown those feelings in bullshit. You'll never deal with them and they'll continue to fester or get you in some shit you can't get out."

"Man, August, I'm aight."

"*Okay*." He exhaled into the phone. "Still, *please*, take it easy. I'll see you in the morning."

"Aight, bet."

Once I ended the call, I peeked at the time on my desk's clock and tapped my finger on my knee cap a few times, thinking.

I heard August, and he was right. The man was very wise and extremely disciplined. Two things I wasn't looking to be that evening.

See, me? I always understood the best way to get over a woman was to get under a new one. Period.

"Fuck it." I planted my feet on the floor and made my way into my bathroom to shower, get dressed, and head out.

———

My *Jaguar XJ's* wheels rolled over strewn branches and fallen leaves as I approached the wrought-iron gates. Two statues, molded into the shape of men and carved out of obsidian, stood on opposite sides of the gated entrance, reflecting glints of light off their hardened surfaces.

I peeked up through my windshield to see the silver moon glowing from the black sky and instantly thought of Leelah.

A flash of the moon cycles wrapped around her ankle came to mind. I glimpsed it when I had her legs in the air a few nights ago. I licked my lips at the thought and shook my head to get her out of my mind. Tonight I couldn't have that woman no where on the brain, not with what I was about to do.

I pulled up to the side of the intercom, inches in front of the gate. Usually I had a driver driving me around town, but I couldn't have him chauffeur me here.

"Password?" the baritone voice echoed through the tiny white intercom.

"Red and gold," I answered.

The gates parted and folded outward, opening up for me. I eased off the brakes, giving my ride a little gas, and the car rolled forward.

A few miles up the road, I spotted the house. Well, really, it was a mansion filled with several outfitted rooms, each as big as one-story homes. Made of sandstone, the chateau towered over everything, even the trees. The property sat on land upon land with not another estate anywhere in sight. It had no street signs because it had no address. You had to use GPS coordinates to get here.

I parked beside a domino line of vehicles and stepped out of my car, adjusting my black tie and then my tailored suit jacket.

The dress code for this spot was formal, no exceptions. On the first Thursday of every month, the paid and open visited here for a night of private clean fun with no rules and right about now, I needed both.

"Welcome to Chateau Luxure, Mr. Williams," a woman greeted the moment I stepped a foot on the first cement paved step.

I nodded at her greeting and she smiled big. She was beautiful. All the women who worked here were. An angled bob framed her slim face, a red formfitting dress outfitted her physique.

"Can I interest you in a glass of champagne?" she asked.

I peeked past her to see a guy dressed in an all-black suit balancing a shiny silver platter in his hand, filled with champagne glasses brimming with the sparkling wine.

"Yeah, thanks." I reached for one once I got to the top of the stairs. "I appreciate it."

"Pryce. Williams." I heard the moment I strode through the doors. My head switched to the left and focused on the woman with the English accent standing at the threshold of her office door. "When they told me to expect your arrival, I made it a priority to greet you myself."

"Mimi." I made my way closer to her. "How you been?"

"Fabulous, of course." She leaned in when I was close and gave me two air kisses. "You look incredibly scrumptious. Every time I see you, I'm impressed with how better you get with time."

"I'll take that as a compliment coming from a woman who does the same."

She pressed her hand to her chest and fluttered her lashes. "And still *oh so* charming too. If I still had the stamina, I'd take you myself."

I chuckled, dipping my hand into the inside pocket of my blazer, and handed her a bulging manila envelope.

"I put a little something extra in there for my perfect getaway."

"You're always spoiling me." She giggled. "Do you need a room? The gold room is vacant."

"Nah." I shook my head and took a sip of my champagne. "I'm here for the atmosphere right now. I'll play it by ear and will give a holla if I need a room."

"Pryce Williams? Here only for the atmosphere?!" She asked, eyes wide. "What's wrong, dear? Are you ill?"

I swallowed back my laugh. "Nah, Mimi, I'm aight. Just focused on chillin' for a bit."

What I wanted to say was my heart was in Tribeca right now, trapped by my first love who wouldn't reciprocate, rightfully so. Oh, and that my ass really shouldn't even be here.

"Well, all right, go on then." She smiled. "Enjoy yourself. You always do."

"Singles Thursday" was a once a month event strictly for the paid and social with sophisticated sexual appetites. Only a select few made it in.

Red carpet stretched out ahead of me while tiny chandeliers led me toward the main ballroom where some of us gathered. The others were in one room watching a live sex show or in the bath house fucking in the sunroof jacuzzi. Now that section of the chateau was a voyeur's dreamland because you could simply look up to watch other people get theirs. Like a porno projected on the ceiling.

Tonight wasn't for the shy. You knew what you were getting into when you paid your fifteen grand at the door and strolled up in here.

I had no business being here, and I knew that. But shit, I needed a distraction. I had to get Leelah off my mind.

Celebrities of all kinds hung out here. From the reality TV stars to the blockbuster movie sirens, they all tiptoed over these floors in search of a good private time.

A lot of paid plain janes and joes coveted this spot, too. If you got wind about the event, got past those iron gates, and could afford to get in, you were here.

The staff at *Chateau Luxure* weren't strangers to hosting sex events. In fact, they held them throughout the year. They dedicated a night to single women, one night a year to married couples, and the first Thursday night of every month was for singles in a particular tax bracket like me. Specifically, here to mingle and fuck anonymously, then forget about it the moment we left through those doors.

Two suited-gentlemen pulled the doors opened for me, nodding their heads my way. What was great about this place was the discretion, although an almost published exposé threatened to compromise the place's anonymity. A reporter was rumored to have shopped the piece around to local newspapers, but no editor would touch it. Mimi, *Chateau's* owner, has friends in high places who made sure the article never saw the light of day.

Neon lights lit up the bar that stretched from one end of the room to the other. Shelves and shelves of liquor lined the real estate behind the bartenders, mostly men, who served wine and other hard liquor to attendees.

"Pryce?" I heard behind me.

When I peeked over my shoulder, I noticed her dark eyes first. They sparkled under the giant chandelier hanging over our heads, the specs of light dancing along her pupils.

"Is that really you?" Mykal asked next.

I brought the rim of my chilled champagne glass to my lips and tossed the sparkling wine back, finishing my drink, and placing the glass atop one table before she arrived in front of me.

"The universe is definitely rewarding me for good behavior," she bragged, her eyes coasting up and down my frame. "You wear a suit so well."

I smiled, my eyes performing its own dance down her shape. "And you wear nude even better."

She wore a form fitting brown dress that wrapped around her body like a rubber band. In the spots where cloth disappeared laid mesh, offering the decadent illusion she was naked. Shorty had a body for days, centuries even, and she was far from shy about showing it off.

Her skin shined as much as her eyes and now her teeth as she smiled big and wide for me.

"You know you're with me tonight, right?" she proposed. "Because there's no way I will allow otherwise."

I smirked. "Is that right?"

She moved in close, balanced her petite frame on the arches of her stilettos and even when she did, she still couldn't reach me, but I loved that she tried.

Right below my lips she whispered, "Hell yeah," then winked.

I licked my lips slow. "Bet."

"I can tell my patience with you is about to pay off."

Mykal had been shooting her shot since my first interview with her a year ago. She was a beautiful woman with stunning eyes, a killer smile, and a body sinful at every curve. She wasn't Leelah, but on some real shit? She would do.

Mykal asked, "Do you have a room?"

"I don't."

"Why not?" she challenged. "You can afford it."

"I came here to chill before deciding to get one."

"Have you been here before?" She exhaled a breathy giggle. "Chill? People come here to *fuck*, Pryce. *Not* chill, handsome."

I snorted a laugh, knowing she was right.

Most guests didn't have rooms. In fact, there was very little available. With the sex shows in one, the orgies in the others, and the stripper parties in the few that remained, vacant rooms were uncommon and given on a first comes, first serve unless you reserved one from ahead of time or paid an extra dollar amount with at least one comma in the price.

"No worries." Mykal dipped her hand into her purse and pulled out a red key. I got the hook up and always have a room on reserve." She grabbed my wrist. "Let's go."

I let her pull me in the direction to exit the ballroom. Allowed it because I had no plans of turning her down. Leelah made it very clear there could be nothing more than the night we hooked up and I was desperate to get her off my mind and out of my system. Our relationship ended over ten years ago and she was still hanging on to shit I did that I couldn't alter. I needed change in my life and fast.

Through the foyer and up the winding stairs, we'd finally reached the red room, one of the few rooms empty for the night.

Mykal glanced at me over her shoulder and smiled before placing her key in the keyhole, turning it, and pushing open the door.

The room was dark, but the moon outside provided enough light. A large canopy bed occupied the center of the room accompanied by two side tables, a box of condoms stationed on one of them.

Mykal adjusted the light's dimmer near the door, illuminating the room only a little. She wasted no time, kicking off her heels and grabbing at one strap of her dress.

"Oh, how rude of me." She stopped and instead let her hands fall at her sides. "I should have asked first. Do you want to take this off me or would you like me to do the honors?"

I exhaled through my mouth, burying my hands in my pockets. "Either way is fine with me."

She smiled, moving her arms behind her to unzip the back of her dress.

Mykal was ready, peeling the straps down her arms and removing the garment entirely. What remained was the sexy matching nude lace undergarments she wore beneath her nude dress.

"Damn, girl," I said, staring at her physique.

Mykal was petite but stacked. What she lacked in height, she made up for in body. Breasts, waist, and ass ratio very proportionate.

"I feel even better," she purred. "Come closer and confirm for yourself."

It was like having cement blocks for feet, that's how heavy they weighed as I ambled over to her. I wasn't close enough when she reached for me and pulled me to her. Her soft hands had a lot of strength in them when she ran her manicured nails down my waist and stopped at my crotch. She held my bulge in her hand and squeezed, and I groaned at her touch.

"*Wow*," she breathed, glimpsing up at me. "And the rumors are true. You can't be real."

I smiled. "You ready for all that?"

"Honestly, I'm unsure." She undid the buckle on my pants slow, her eyes still on me. "The best way to find out is for me to go in."

I closed my eyes, forcing myself in the moment as she progressed to the button and zipper of my slacks. But the moment my lids shut, all I could see was Leelah. Her sex faces, how she smelled that night we hooked up after all those years of being apart. The glide of her soft hands up my arm, against my back.

Leelah moved like fucking magic beneath me, on top of me, and in front of me, man, everywhere I twisted her. She offered that spark, that zing, I hadn't experienced in years. My breaths were easier to take with her. Lying with her afterwards was like sleeping on the finest cloud.

I grabbed Mykal by her wrist when she dipped her hand into my boxers, stopping her descent toward my dick.

"What?" she asked. "Don't tell me you're one of those types who don't enjoy receiving head."

"Nah, sweetheart." I licked my lips. "That's the last thing I am."

She bit her bottom lip nervously, her brows furrowing. "So... what's up?"

I shut my eyes tight then reopened them, and she sighed heavily.

"*Noooo*," she whined. "*Please* no."

"I'm sorry sweetheart," I apologized, stepping back, zipping my pants. "It's not you though."

My eyes rolled down her form as I buttoned and buckled my slacks. It most definitely *wasn't* her. Mykal's body was banging. It glistened under the dimmed lighting and was calling my name, begging for me to answer. Her scent was enticing. She was ready. But she wasn't Leelah, and that shit was fucking with something deep in me hard. And not in a good way.

"It's Ms. Phone Call, isn't it?" she quizzed. "The person you were on the phone with after your interview with me? The one who had you damn near hopping on the balls of your feet with a smile so big you'd think she was Vegas itself calling?"

I snorted a laugh, and she smiled.

"Yeah," I answered. "It is."

"Okay, now I *really* hate her." Mykal dropped her head back between her shoulders and grunted. "My life. So close to fucking Pryce Williams." She grunted again, this time louder. "You know that will go in my obituary, right?"

I laughed out loud, and she joined me then rolled her eyes.

"Fine, go," she forced out. Mykal made her way over to the bed and climbed on, throwing her back against the mattress. "Run to the girl who puts the bounce in your step and the air in your fine ass wings. I guess I'll be using my fingers tonight."

"I apologize," I said, "sincerely I do."

"It's okay," she replied. "I mean it's not okay, but I understand. At least it's because you love this woman and not because I'm not hot, because I'm hot. I'd fuck me tonight, shit."

"Yeah, you're hot sweetheart." I licked my lips. "You hot as hell."

Even in the dimmed room, I could see her fighting back her smile.

I turned to leave.

When I reached in front of the door, turning the knob to open it, I twisted my head to glance her way and told her, "If it's any consolation..."

"Uh-huh?"

"If this was a year ago, I would've fucked you so good you'd have no voice to even take phone calls at work the next day."

She rolled her eyes closed, sighed, then laid flat on her back, spreading her legs wide.

"You tell me that now? Fucking tease," she said, sliding her hands to her pussy. "Close the door, Pryce, unless of course you want to watch."

I snickered to myself and stepped out, closing the door behind me.

———

Closing one door only to stand in front of another?

I have no idea what I was thinking, what I was even doing in front of this door.

The thing is... I couldn't think of any other place to be. I blew fifteen grand at a spot where I only drank champagne, all because I couldn't get Leelah off my mind.

What should have happened was, I should have taken my ass home after leaving *Chateau Luxure*. But instead, I stood on the threshold of Leelah's loft after getting the okay from her doorman to just go up the moment I waltzed through the lobby's turnstile entrance.

I knocked four times and stepped back, waiting.

Shortly after, I heard, "Pryce?" on the other end.

I said nothing.

She pulled open the door and my eyes immediately fell on her black and pink floral kimono.

"I'm going to have to talk to my doorman," she whispered to herself.

Her gray eyes were red rimmed, like she'd been crying. Her lips in a pout. She looked like how I was feeling, that's how I knew something deeper connected us.

I approached her door, and she didn't move away, only stood there, her head falling back to keep her eyes on me.

"What's up?" I said to her.

"Nothing much," she replied.

I wet my lips with my whole tongue and heard when she exhaled below me.

"Can I come in?"

Her eyes darted along mine and her lips parted, but nothing came out.

I brought my hands to the V between her thighs, and she gasped.

"Here." I told her. "I want to come in *here*."

Before she could respond, I crushed my lips against hers and slipped her my tongue, which she received and reciprocated by giving me hers.

I lifted her up with one hand, then kicked the door closed behind me, wrapping her legs around my waist while carrying her up to her bedroom.

She moaned on my lips and held me tight, her eyelids shut tighter.

In her room, we fell on the bed together. Her hands were at my tie undoing it, mine at her waist releasing the knot on the belt of her kimono. She undid the buttons of my shirt so fast that I hadn't noticed when she progressed to my belt buckle or the button on my pants.

I dipped my hand into my pocket, pulled out a condom and struggled to rip it open with my teeth. She snatched it from me, brought it to her mouth and tore it open with ease.

With the condom free and my erection out of my pants, she reached down between us, rolled the condom on in expert speed, and guided me inside of her.

We both gasped at the point of penetration. Her robe laid at her sides, her arms still in the sleeves. My pants were down at my ankles, shirt opened, my tie somewhere I didn't care. I couldn't care less about anything outside of her.

I pumped in and out of her with abandon, filling her, witnessing as her walls opened up for me quicker this time with each thrust.

"*Yes*, fuck me tonight, Pryce," she whispered. "I don't want it slow."

Neither did I. So I kept at it. Gave her everything. All the anger with myself for my fuck up and the wasted years, and her stalling to take me back. I fucked her like it was the last night on earth and I had to make her feel everything I couldn't say before the world ended.

She hollered her pleasure, clawed her nails down the back of my shirt. I watched her drag her bottom lip between her teeth when I found her spot and banged at it, refusing to let up off it.

"Pryce!" she screamed, her eyes locked on mine.

"I fucking love you," I breathed out. "Know that, aight? I love you *so* much, La."

When I pulled out of her, she refused to let me go. I grabbed her by one thigh and turned her over. She laid flat on her stomach when I plunged into her again, and she ground out my name once more through her teeth.

Our breathing was a chorus of exhaustion, the both of us trying our hardest to keep up.

The room was dark but still lit by the moon lamp on her table. A small ball of light, changing from pure white to orange. Leelah always loved moons, and they reminded me of her every time I saw one.

I fisted her curls, pulled her up on her knees and pounded into her. Leelah's leather headboard rattled against the cement wall as I worked her over with no mercy, grabbing her by the wrists and handcuffing them with my hand to fuck her at an angle so she'd feel the drive of each thrust. I had to give it to her how we both needed it and then some.

I'd give the world to her if she wanted it. I'd give her anything in that moment and for life if she let me.

The fluttering of her walls hinted she was close, so did her sudden silence. Leelah always made it easy to tell she was coming because her moans would always come to a sudden halt all so she could focus on meeting her orgasm head on.

"I feel it too," I whispered to her, my hands releasing her wrists and smoothing down to her breasts to hold. "I feel you coming with me, baby."

We shook together, our bodies finding it impossible to hold us up against gravity or to continue.

"Whatever fool lucky enough to get you after tonight," I exhaled. "I'm gonna give him a hard fucking time whenever I'm in town, I promise you."

She grabbed the bedsheets in her hand and held the fabric in her grip as her ass clapped against my pelvis.

"You won't consider him to be enough, anyway," I forecasted through my teeth. "Because he won't be me and I'm who's best for you."

"Christ," she whispered.

"You're my forever," I strained, feeling the stress of the cords in my neck standing out. "'Cause you got my heart and I don't want that shit back from you. No matter what you think, what you believe. *You* are my end goal." I grabbed her by her forearms, folding them over her lower back and locking them together, pumping harder. She dropped her face into the sheets in response. "So come and find me when you're ready. You hear me?"

Her legs trembled beneath me, but I never faltered.

"Come and find me," I repeated, dropping my head back between my shoulders. "'Cause I'll be waiting on you."

A rush of energy surged from the pads of my heels to the top of my head. Every muscle in my body locked in place as I braced myself to come. My grip tightened on her arms, my teeth bit down on my bottom lip so hard I almost broke skin. And when it hit, I roared my release into the surrounding space and she whimpered hers. I released my grip on her arms to lean forward and to press my hands to the wall above her headboard for balance. She disconnected and fell to her side on the bed.

Leelah rolled over, her body glistening below me. Breasts in full view, her pussy still spasming, I could tell from the twitching her lower lips did. Leelah ran her palm down her face to clean it of her sweat as she stared up at me.

"I'm..." I told her through my breaths. "I'm going back to Oakland."

Still breathing hard, she balanced herself on her elbows to peer up at me with shock in her eyes, but she said nothing.

"And I'm leaving this Sunday."

Her lips trembled and her eyes instantly became wet.

The moment I saw that, I thought for sure she'd beg me to stay. Tell me she reconsidered and pull me close, telling me she could never let me go again.

But instead she bobbled her head up and down with tears in her eyes and whispered, "Okay."

SEVENTEEN

"Can I start you two off with anything?" the long-haired, bright eyed waitress quizzed as she stood over our table.

My sister Gena and I had taken our seats at *Pho* - an upscale Asian bistro in the Meatpacking District, only ten minutes away from my loft. It was a Saturday night, a little after 9 p.m., and the restaurant hummed with energy.

"Give us a moment to review the menu," Gena replied, and the waitress nodded her exit.

"I feel loved," I taunted with a smirk. "She invited me out to a place where they'll be serving us for a change and not a bar where we need to yell our orders at a bartender."

She scoffed a laugh. "Whatever smart ass."

I giggled.

"I came here with Fenton last week and thought you'd love this place."

"There goes that name again." I dropped my eyes down on my menu. "More than once raises my antennas."

"Like I said, he's cool."

"And what you didn't say is that he's still putting it down like no other has ever."

My sister cackled.

"Because the Gena *I* know through and through doesn't talk this much about a *blind date* the way she's been gushing over Mr. Black Ken Barbie."

When she had said nothing, I peeked up from my menu to find her smiling sweetly in her seat.

"Aw, shit!"

She pointed at me. "Do not start Leelah."

"*Damn Gena!*" I yelled in my Martin Lawrence impersonation. "You are so sprung."

A laugh ripped from her gut and bellowed out her mouth as she lightly kicked me beneath the table.

"*Shh,*" she shushed while stealing a glance around herself. "Would you stop making a damn spectacle, La?"

"Okay, Fenton." I slow clapped, ignoring her. "Got my big sister all smitten in public. I can get with that."

"Stop making a big deal out of nothing." She smiled.

"I just mentioned that man's name and your whole face lit up like a supernova. If he can do that, he's okay with me." I winked. "I love seeing you like this G, seriously."

Gena waved her hand in the air. "Let's not get ahead of ourselves, okay? It's been nice so far. He's cool."

"*He's cool,*" I mimicked. "Well, alrighty then. I'm still super happy for you two."

"I'm just ready," she confirmed, smiling. "Ready to be open-hearted and a little vulnerable for a change."

I nodded in an attempt to relate.

"If only things would have worked out for you and Marshall..."

I gagged, and she snickered.

"Speaking of things working out though." She tilted her head to the side, and I already understood where this conversation was veering.

As a result, my smile slid off my face.

I'd finally found a moment to take my mind off my reality. Thursday night was one of the hardest nights to fall asleep.

After Pryce left my place post-coital, I cried my ass to slumber like a baby. Pride kept me from telling him what was really on my heart. I wanted to tell him to not go and to stay there with me for more than a night. Indefinitely. To make me forget the shit he did because I fucking loved him so much too.

Him being back in my life for the short time he'd returned took me on a roller coaster of emotions. First, it pissed me off that he thought he could pop back into my life when he wanted, like some jack-in-the-box. Then I was disappointed when he decided to not over extend his welcome and to head back to the place that kept him from me for over ten years.

The situation left me conflicted. Conflicted had been my new normal since he returned in my life, and I couldn't shake the feeling.

"Leelah," Gena said across from me.

I pressed my fingertips to my eyelashes, not caring about smearing my mascara. It was a few seconds away from raining down my cheeks, anyway.

"What *happened*?" she asked, already knowing.

"He's going back to Oakland."

She cringed, squeezing her eyes closed.

"He came over Thursday night and we hooked up again and right after, he told me he was heading back."

"No." She shook her head. "This is not the way this story should end."

I shrugged.

"Can I get you started on anything yet—"

"Get away from our table!" Gena spat.

My jaw dropped.

Gena cupped her mouth with her hand while raising her other hand apologetically to the waitress whose eyes widened about two sizes bigger like they were a few seconds away from popping out of her head. "I am *so* sorry. We..." My sister gestured between us. "... are talking about something life changing right now. If you can give us five more minutes, I promise, we'll be ready to order."

The waitress nodded and turned to leave the table again.

"Sheesh," I said.

"*Sheesh* right back at you."

"Look," I began, "I sympathize with you and you wanting floor seats at *Ballers* games and all—"

"It's more than the floor seats, baby sis," she interjected. "I mean yes, floor seats would have been the shit, but your heart means more than that to me."

"My heart... is fine."

"No it's not."

"Pryce and I were years ago."

"And yet you haven't gotten over him. Not even an iota."

I rolled my eyes.

She leaned over her empty plate, placing her elbows on the table. "He fucked up. What he did to you when you two were younger was fucked up, and that's a fact. But he wants back in and he's not looking to get back in giving you the old Pryce. And based on what you've told me, the things he's said to you since he's been back, he's holding his heart in his hand for you. People can grow from their mistakes, Leelah. They *can* learn a lot from their bullshit. And some people *do* deserve second chances if they've showed you change."

"I know," I said low. "It isn't him at this point, it's me."

She wrinkled her brows.

"I felt like I had something to prove. Show him he can't step back into my life and think that I've been waiting for him."

A smile crested her lips. "But you *have* been waiting for him. You may not realize it Leelah but that's exactly what you've been doing this whole time."

I remained silent.

"Pryce has always been that guy for you. Just the mention of his name before he stepped back into your life would turn your smile into a frown. But I've watched you these past few days, especially after your hookup with him. You've had a different glow about you."

I bit back my smile.

"You still love him just as much as he loves you, perhaps even more."

"I *do*."

"So fuck the past, La. Just fuck it!"

I shook my head.

"I'm not saying to forget it and pretend like it never happened, but

Pryce has shown and proved that he is a different man. He's owned up to his fuck up and I'm sure is showing that he wants more than what's between your legs."

"He has."

"And honestly?" She smiled nervously, "I *really* do want those damn floor seats. Like I want them so bad I can already feel the wind blowing through my hair as the players run up and down the court. I can't even lie to you, La."

I snorted a giggle, which turned into a full-blown laugh that bellowed from my gut. "You fool."

"I'm being honest!" she cheesed. "My baby sister, the boo of *NBA's* finest who's playing for the *Bronx Ballers*! My favorite team of all time?!" She dropped her head back between her shoulders. "Yeah, a fucking dream come true."

"Dare to dream," I teased.

"Nope, it's going to happen." She pointed at me. "Because I know you will do the right thing. I raised you to always do the right thing."

"Shut up! *You raised me*, psh."

She laughed.

I spotted the waitress approaching our table from the corner of my eye.

"Are you two ready *now*?" she asked once she arrived in front of our table, a smile plastered to her lips.

"I know I'm ready." Gena pointed her eyes at me, wiggling her brows. "Are you finally ready too, Leelah?"

It was clear her question superseded the subject of food in that instance. I bit my lip while nodding. "Yeah, I think I might be ready too."

Eighteen

"You have an interview with *The Sports Report* tomorrow morning," Marc reminded.

I focused my eyes out of my window, my chin balanced in my palm as we rode in the back seat of a black SUV headed to a private airport to fly out to California. The afternoon was cloudy, no sun in sight, the perfect way to leave the east coast. Especially with how I was feeling.

"*For The Culture* sent the layout from the interview for you to review," Marc continued. "The photos came out good, my man. They're thinking about putting you on the cover for a future issue."

I grunted.

"Yo, Pryce," Marc said beside me. "You aight?"

I kissed my teeth. "You know I ain't *aight*, man."

He sighed.

"Look, P." He tapped my arm with the back of his hand to get my attention. "Am I happy that we're going back? Not exactly. Not at all, actually. I found this dope ass condo in the Upper West Side with views my dude and a fine ass single neighbor who thinks *my* ass is cute. Can you believe that?"

I snorted a laugh.

"But what else is there for us to do here?"

I shrugged.

"Do you want to sign with the *Ballers*? Their offer is more than the *Flames*, although the *Flames* have promised to match it."

"Nah." My eyes shifted down to my lap. "I can't stay out here if I'm not with her. It'll be fucking torture. Me constantly telling her how I feel and her never reciprocating because she can't get over old shit and rightfully so." I shook my head. "Nah, I gotta go."

Marc nodded.

I leaned back a bit in my seat, stretching my legs and pushing my hand into my pocket in search of my phone.

"Shit!"

"What?" Marc asked.

"I left my phone at the loft."

"Darnell got it," Marc confirmed. "He texted me about it a moment ago. Said he'll have it for you by tomorrow when he arrives in Cali."

I ran my hand down the length of my face. "Great, fucking great."

I pressed my head against the headrest of my seat and closed my eyes. Her face faded into memory. The sea of tears around her eyes when I told her I was leaving. There was something different though, like she didn't want me to go. But that never translated to words. Leelah let me leave her place, saying nothing besides *"okay."* That shit hurt. It hurt because I'd put my heart out there. Apologized for the shit I did and gave her my word that I would never make the same stupid decision again to play with her heart, and it wasn't enough... again, rightfully so. She had every right to feel how she felt. I just wish things were different. I'd give anything for everything to work out differently between us this time.

"Hold up," Marc announced beside me. "Is that Leelah?"

My head slung forward, moving from side to side, my eyes going wild to catch the same view.

"Where?" I asked.

Marc pointed out the side of his window. "Yo! That is her by the gate. What is she—"

"Stop the truck! I yelled.

"Sir?" the driver questioned, peeking at me through the rear-view mirror.

"I need to get out," I clarified.

"Mr. Williams, you can not exit the vehicle at this part of the airport," he explained. "This is the entrance. Stopping will obstruct traffic."

I flipped the lock and pulled open the door while the SUV was still in motion.

"Yo!" Marc yelled. "Let the truck stop first, damn."

The driver stomped on the brakes, forcing the truck into a screeching abrupt stop.

My feet were on the paved road before he could put the vehicle in park.

I jogged toward her, refusing to waste time walking.

She stood near the front gate in only a t-shirt, jeans, and a pair of sneakers, her hands hidden in her back pockets.

As I raced toward her, I noticed she wore a vintage *Bronx Ballers* tee. I laughed, covering my mouth with a fist.

"I called your phone but Darnell said you'd forgotten it," she quipped when I was close. "He told me where you were flying out, so I thought I'd swing by."

"Oh you thought you'd swing by, huh?" I asked in front of her. "For what?"

She dropped her eyes to the ground, then focused up at me again. "I was thinking..."

I couldn't contain my smile or my racing heart. "What you was thinking about?"

She ran her fingers through her long curls and smiled back. "That the *Bronx Ballers* aren't *so* bad."

I cringed and admitted low, "They would have to be a little better to be at least bad, La. And that's me being nice."

She forced back her laugh. "But something tells me their stats are about to improve this season."

"Yeah, with you wearing their shirt as fine as you are."

She blushed.

We stared at each other for a moment, our eyes doing most of the talking until she said, "Don't go."

I released all the air in me, relief washing over me, cleansing me of all the doubt I'd had since flying back to New York for the summer.

"Dad and Gena really want *Bronx Ballers* floor seats."

I laughed and so did she.

"And what do *you* want?"

Private planes took off in the distance, creating a noisy background for our exchange. But I still heard when she answered with, "Us."

I closed my eyes and had to keep myself from screaming my joy, my thanks. It was finally happening. Late, but still on time.

"So, what you're saying is...?" I moved in closer and took her hand. Her head fell back to gaze up at me. "You and me again?"

Leelah smiled so wide, laugh lines framed her lips.

She said, "Yeah, part deux."

I squeezed my eyes shut and whispered, "Yes!"

She snorted.

"And the sequel will be well worth the second chance, baby, I swear."

I stepped closer to her and took her chin in my hand, lowering my lips to hers.

"Under one condition," she proffered before I could kiss her.

"And what's that?"

"We both take an oath of abstinence before marriage."

I groaned all the air out of me, and this made her laugh. "Leelah, no, *please*, no, no, no, *nooo*!"

"I got to do this for me," she replied, her gray eyes fixed on me. "I made a promise to myself that I would maintain my chastity until my wedding night and although I broke that with you, I want to make another promise and keep it this time, Pryce."

I dropped my head back between my shoulders. "Oh, sweet lord."

"And..." She wrapped her arms around my waist, making me lower my gaze to her. "I want you to do this with me. I think it'll be beneficial for the both of us."

"Beneficial? How baby, how?! We've already done *it*."

"We'll get to know each other again. The new us." She licked her lips. "Help me build back my trust with you. It'll be like high school. Sex has a way with creating blurred lines. The physical connection can be like a substitute for deep affection and I want only clarity with you moving forward. Besides, your patience back in the day was *so* sexy and I want to experience that again with you."

I sighed in defeat.

"And I promise I'll be worth the wait."

"Oh, I already know that's a fact," I replied, running my hand down my beard while looking away.

"Plus," she added, turning my face by the chin to focus on her again. "You said that I should tell you what you have to do to get back here." She placed my hand at her heart. "Well, *this* is what you have to do, okay?"

I ran my hand down my beard a second time, swallowed hard, then sighed again. "Aight, La, if that's what you want from me, baby, then let's do it."

She showed all her teeth in that moment. "Really?!"

I nodded. "Hell yeah, really."

She threw her arms around my neck and pulled me down into a kiss. Her lips were so soft against mine, plump with so much emotion and passion, I felt like I was floating when I met her tongue with mine.

"Yeah, boy!" Marc yelled from the truck, his head poking out of the window. "Get all up in there, Pryce!"

Leelah and I laughed on each other's lips then shouted, "Shut up, Marc!"

I couldn't believe it, I actually did it. I finally got my girl back in my arms and she had returned to me even sexier, abundantly smarter, and with the kind of moves to make my toes curl in bed. Leelah was now the entire package, but the thing I desired the most from her was far from anything physical. It was her heart, the only part of her that has always mattered the most and that I'd been wanting to reclaim, with her blessing. I planned to protect it and this love I'd regained with everything in me. There was no way I was fucking this up again. *No* way.

Just thinking about our future left me stoked. Not only did my life finally make sense again, it was about to be so lit with my woman by my side, and for life this time.

EPILOGUE
ONE YEAR LATER...

LEELAH

"By the power vested in me," the pastor proclaimed with the sun setting in the background, "I now pronounce you husband and wife."

I lifted my gaze to Pryce and winked.

"You may now kiss your bride."

We stood opposite one another below an awning made of white peonies on *Guana Island*. Surrounded by only a handful of our friends and family, Pryce stepped forward and into my space.

I'm sure my smile sparkled beneath the orange sunlight when he pulled me close by the waist.

Dreaming about this moment for months was my norm. Literally fantasizing about the moment we'd profess our love in front of the people whom we loved was what fueled me every day.

I giggled as he licked his lips slowly and lowered them to mine. Pressing my hands to his cheeks, he met my lips with his.

Our guests applauded our intimate act that Pryce and I refused to let up off of.

"Yessss!" Gena yelled from her seat, her fingers no doubt interlocked with her boyfriend, Fenton's. "Get it, girl."

Pryce's best friend and manager, Marc, clapped and hooted from his seat not too far from my sister's.

Both Pryce and I laughed on each other's lips at their reactions while still indulging on one another for just another moment. I refused to get enough of him. And after all this waiting, I was ready to return to the other place that gave me joy: on top of him.

The year of abstinence was a challenging one for the both of us, but we kept our promise and were ready to unwrap our reward for waiting.

Five months after agreeing to give us another chance, Pryce asked me to be his wife, down on one knee at the dinner table at my dad's house. The man could have orchestrated an elaborate over the top proposal, but he chose to keep it intimate with my family. That won me over completely.

On the career front, Pryce had just completed his first season as a *Bronx Baller,* getting the team that ring they've been pining over for the past few years. In public, he credited focus, teamwork, and dedication as the reason he along with his teammates brought the *Ballers* to the finals. In private with me though, he confessed that not having sex for all those months added to his aggression and laser focus on the court. Whatever it was, the press heralded Pryce as the *Ballers'* savior. He planned to remain on the team until his retirement next year.

Moments after exchanging vows, we joined our friends and family for an intimate dinner on the beach.

Before we took our seats to eat our meals, we swayed in each other's arms to Tamia and Eric Benét's "Spend My Life With You" for our first dance. After, we dined on succulent lobster tails and sipped on chilled premium champagne during the dinner course.

Sitting beside each other at our sweetheart table made entirely of fragrant red roses, Pryce leaned closer to me, his hand sliding up my thigh and past the slit of my off-the-shoulder white lace dress. His hands left trails of heat against my skin, mapping his journey upward.

I caught his hand just before his fingers reached for the seat of my panties.

"Not yet," I whispered.

He breathed in my ear and said, "I swear on everything holy I can't wait any longer, wifey. I'm ready to take you down right now."

I turned to kiss him on the tip of his nose. "You've waited this long. What's another hour?"

———

PRYCE

Another hour was like another year, but she was right, I'd been patient for that long, I could extend the wait for a little longer. Once that hour was up, she and I excused ourselves from the party to head up to our room.

We stood on the threshold of our suite, my heart racing, hands feigned out to feel her in the nude. Leelah took but a few steps into the room when I scooped her up in my arms and tossed her over my shoulder.

"Pryce!"

"Pryce, what?"

In my view was the bed. A dope California king covered in so many red rose petals shaped into a heart, I couldn't make out the sheets beneath them.

In front of the bed, I dropped her down onto her back, the roses billowing up then scattering to the floor.

The private resort outfitted the room in gold and wicker. The canopy bed Leelah now laid on had a shelf headboard, where a vase of two dozen red roses decorated the surface. Gold railings around the bed and a sheer white curtain pinned at the top accentuated the bed's allure.

I peeled off my white linen shirt and damn near ripped off the matching shorts.

"Aren't you going to romance me first?" she teased.

"I sure as hell am not, Dr. Williams. We're *fucking* tonight. You and I have a whole lifetime for me to romance you. Tonight, though, we put in some work. Now, come here."

It took a little convincing for Leelah to drop her maiden name and to take my surname. I didn't push her on it, although I really wanted her to have it. But with some begging on my part, she changed her name with jubilation.

"*Aww*, I love the sound of that..." She blushed. "... Dr. Williams."

"I got something else for you to love." I pulled out my dick and held it in my hand.

She moaned at the sight of it, bringing her fingertips to the head to caress. "I'm not getting any sleep tonight, am I?"

"None," I confirmed, right before I pounced.

Our abstinence pack was like a slow death for me. There, I said it. The oath she and I promised to maintain had a few touch and go moments. One of which included me flying in from a game in Minnesota, begging her down on my knees to concede at three in the morning. Blue balls became a common occurrence for me, and cold showers were a major staple of my day. But we made it to our version of the finals, our wedding day, and I got the ring I really wanted. And from the sex in my wife's eyes as I watched her survey my torso, Leelah was more than willing to show her appreciation for my obedience.

Her practice had been booming ever since the press linked her to what people have resorted to calling me – the *NBA's* golden boy. She was a year booked out and people were still dialing her office number to get an appointment with her.

I was one of her clients. In addition to abstinence, one of her other requests was that we sort through my past relationship with my neighbor and my mother. Turns out I didn't have a sex addiction, but I did have self-image issues linked to my mother leaving me so young. I was projecting, relying on the attention of women and the intimacy sex provided. I realized I'd been using those things to fill the void and to replace the absence of the one woman who left, to the point of carelessly hurting the one person who truly loved me for me - Leelah. One of the things Leelah had me do was reach out to my mother and truly express how I felt about her bouncing when I was a child. The conversation was raw and uncomfortable, but therapeutic. It lifted weight off me I didn't even realize I'd been carrying. I learned my mother had a lot of growing to do in her youth and just wasn't ready to parent. Although that didn't do anything for my past, it helped it make sense and made me want to be a better parent to my kids. My mother and my relationship didn't miraculously improve after that conversation, I still kept her at a distance, but at least my wonderment of why she left and if it was because of me was answered. It also helped remove a block I didn't even know I had in my heart so that I could love Leelah fully, without any hang ups.

My life was finally the life of my dreams, a life of bliss. Everything was finally perfect. Not only perfect on the surface but deep down inside perfect, no filter needed.

———

LEELAH

Perfect couldn't even describe where life was these days. No longer did my heart ache about yesteryears. I had my man, and he had his woman.

Pryce grabbed me by the waist, swiped his free hand behind me, knocking the vase of flowers off the bed's shelf and onto the floor and brought me to the shelf headboard of the bed, sitting me on top. He hiked my dress up by the hem, moved the seat of my pure white lingerie to the side, and slid in, his hand pressed against the wall behind my head.

"*Mmm*," I moaned.

"God," he whispered. "I've missed this so much, *fuck*."

He held one of my legs up by the nook of my knee and balanced my leg on his forearm. Served me everything he had and that he'd been wanting to give from the moment I agreed to be his again.

"What did I tell you?" I whispered, running my hand down his cheek. "Didn't I tell you I'd be worth the wait?"

He was so caught up, barely able to keep his eyes opened as he pumped his waist back and forth, losing himself in me. Only able to reply with a nod in that moment.

Pryce slung his head back, his bottom lip held between the bite of his teeth. He finally released his lip long enough to admit, "I never doubted the wait. Not even once."

I got past the sweet ache of his entrance quick. What Pryce didn't know is I was more eager to reunite between the sheets than he was. But I couldn't tell him that. Any sign of wanting to give in would have weakened his resolve, and I wanted us to get through it together, no hiccups.

He leveled his head with mine, leaned in, and slipped me his tongue. We rocked together atop the shelf headboard, my waist sliding down every so often and him catching me, never breaking momentum or losing his pace.

On the third tap against that spot that made me shake, I screamed my delight, and he groaned at the sound of me enjoying him.

"I love you," he avowed on my lips.

"I love *you*," I said back.

We rocked and rolled, then rocked and rolled some more until the evidence of our efforts echoed off the walls and shook the bed beneath us.

I shut my lids tight, my eyes seeing colors I'd never seen, my core throbbing and walls fluttering as I spiraled through my release. Pryce grunted with each stroke he had left in him, his back bucking, hand slamming against the wall behind me for stability as he faltered to a stop.

When we finally slinked down off the headboard and off our afterglow high, I inhaled the surrounding air in the room and smiled to myself. Sated couldn't begin to describe the sensation coursing through me.

On the mattress covered in red roses, we turned our heads to concentrate on one another. I reached for Pryce and he moved in closer until our lips were against each other again. Lost in another lip-lock, we inhaled one another's exhales, knowing we could stay here forever, and excited that we had a second chance to be here again.

Part deux was definitely the shit because in the sequel of our love, Pryce had returned to me as the man of my dreams and my fantasies. Most importantly, he'd returned as a man who I could trust my heart with this time. And for that, he was absolutely worth forgiving and unintentionally waiting for.

THE END.

AUTHOR'S NOTE

Dear Reader:

Thank you so much for reading *LUST*! It's the second book in a series that took me two years to develop and it almost feels surreal finally being able to share it with you.

So we're two books into the series, and I think you get the gist of what this series is all about. *LUST* was one of my favorite books to write because it's a second chance romance and I just love writing those. What I also loved about this book was the redemption element. Pryce had a lot of growing up to do when he wanted a spot back in Leelah's life. Though sometimes his decisions to get back in good with her were a little selfish, they came from a place of wanting to offer his best while apologizing for his worst and assuring he was ready to come correct no matter what it took to do so. But he did more. He also admitted fault, acknowledged Leelah's feelings in the matter, and he did all he could do to get her back, including meeting and satisfying her terms for forgiveness. He did the work, even accepting Leelah's help in evaluating the underlining self-image issues that contributed to his lustful ways.

The most admirable thing, at least what I believe was admirable, was that when he wanted her back, he didn't just say it – he came back ready.

Because saying you're sorry is one thing, right? But showing up and showing you've changed is another.

I'm glad you finally got to meet him. I'd been adding him to a few books before this one if you've noticed - a mention in *Last Comes Love*, another mention in Jaleel Gordon's story *Home For Christmas*, and then actually adding Pryce in a scene in August & Genesis book, *Meant To Be*. Honestly, his inclusion in *Meant To Be* was just so you could see where his head was at before he decided to get his love life together.

For Lealah's character I wanted to create someone who seemingly had everything together on the surface but who was still figuring things out. A therapist seeing a therapist, hint, hint. She's a lot like the strong friend, the one who has the answer to everyone's problems but not a single clue as to how to solve her own. And that makes her a good kind of vulnerable, the type we can relate to and can't help but to see ourselves in. I loved that she was a woman who was in love with love, got disappointed with love, but who deep in her heart of hearts still believed in love although she seemed jaded at times.

Leelah and Pryce will show up in a future book (or books) in the series. Mykal Jones, the journalist who shot her shot and missed with Pryce, and who is also the younger cousin of Amir Jones (*Girl Code & Mr. Mrs. Jones*), she has her own book in the series, *ENVY*, that I'm sure you'll love! For now though, let me know your thoughts on book two, *LUST*, in the Love is Cure series with a review. I'd love to read your thoughts. Oh, but before you do that, be sure to check out chapter one from the next book in the series, *GREED*. I added it to the end of this book!

If this is your first time reading a book by me, thank you for taking a chance and I hope you enjoyed yourself. If you did, you're what I like to call a Brookelynite, welcome! If you're a loyal reader who has been rocking with me from a book, two books, or many books ago, I am so grateful for your continued support. It's my soul food. Whether you're new or a loyal reader of mine, thank you so much for reading. I appreciate you. I write because I love it, but I also write for your love of reading. See you at the end of the next book.

Love,

Brookelyn.

BONUS! CHAPTER ONE FROM GREED

BRYANT

Manhattan, December 16, 2019

"Grandmother, how are you this morning?"

I leaned back in my leather office chair, fingers stroking the fine hairs of my goatee. I'd been practicing this phone call in the mirror for a week.

"Great, Bryant. I'm great," she chirped. "Thanks so much for asking. I'm so happy you called too."

I smiled.

"It's so good to hear your voice. I hardly hear it as often."

"Yeah..." My eyes shifted over to my office windows. "It's been an awfully busy few months for me."

I wasn't lying about that part. As the CEO of a multitude of companies, I barely had enough time to sleep. But I wasn't complaining in the least. This is the life I've always wanted. Built from the ground up by me. Of course I got a familial boost along the way, but all that Bryant Greene earned, Bryant Greene acquired himself.

"Well, that I can believe." She giggled. "How's the salt factory and flour mill holding up? I haven't visited in ages."

"Great!" I moved my view along the edges of my custom made L-shaped office desk. "We've just installed a few more machines to expedite the milling process at the flour mill and have signed fifteen new contracts with gourmet markets to place our salt on their shelves. We're also in talks with a bread company. They're interested in us being a salt supplier for their products."

"Oh, Bryant, that is marvelous news! Your grandfather would be so proud."

I beamed, pleased with the verbal pat on the back.

"You know, when he gifted you the flour mill and salt factory, everyone thought he was insane to do so to a 17-year-old, but I trusted his vision when he noticed something in you that others hadn't yet."

"That he did."

"Now look at you; a billionaire. My grandson is a billionaire. Oh, the heavens!"

I adjusted the knot of my tie. "Well, grandmother, if you really want to brag, they're calling me a multi-billionaire now."

She laughed a hearty laugh and squealed. I couldn't help but to laugh too.

Truthfully, I didn't have the multi-billions in my literal possession but my companies, investments, and overall net worth had reached the $6.1 billion calculation and the year hadn't even ended yet.

"Anyway," she said, clearing her throat, "My busy grandson did not just call to shoot the breeze with this old lady, so what do I owe the pleasure of this phone call?"

"Grandmother, come on now." I chuckled. "Of course I only called to speak with my grandmother. I haven't spoken to you in months."

I hoped like hell that was convincing enough. She knew her grandson well. As soothing as it was, I absolutely didn't call just to hear her voice. My dear ol' granny was sitting on my next money move - land in a prime real estate location in Upstate New York. Morgansville had become a prime real estate location overnight, and I wanted in. Buildings were going up all over that compact town. Condominiums and palatial mansions. It was a predominantly black area, but investors had other plans.

"Aw, Bryant, that is so sweet to think of your grandmother. You have always been my favorite you handsome devil you."

I could feel her smiling on the other end of my phone.

Perfect.

"So, uh, grandmother, tell me, how are things?"

"Fabulous," she gushed. "Simply fabulous! After your cousin's wedding, I have plans to charter a flight to Ghana with a few girl-friends."

"Nice." I nodded slowly, impressed. "Ghana is beautiful."

"Isn't it?! Oh, Bryant, you must go sometime soon. You work so hard. You deserve to treat yourself to a little getaway."

"This is true."

"But before I even leave, I must complete the renovations of the extra room I'm building in the mansion. A little girl cave I've been craving since the summer."

"Girl cave, huh?" I chuckled. "So, uh, on the subject of reno-vations..."

"Mm-hmm...?"

I closed one eye and asked, "How's the property in Morgansville going?"

"*Hmmm...* Morgansville, Morgansville," she repeated to herself, something she often did when she tried recalling something she'd forgotten. "Oh, Morgansville! Wow. I've forgotten all about that old thing. It's well, I suppose."

Yes, I mouthed.

"You suppose?" I questioned. "You don't check up on it?"

"Well, no. Can't even remember the last time I've seen it. Now trust me, the property means plenty to me, but sadly, I hardly visit."

"Hmph." I drummed a rhythm on my desk with my fingertips and counted the seconds before going in for the kill. "You know I can manage it."

"Hmm, would you? It's such an old property, Bryant, nothing like the properties you're used to working with. The property and land it's built on means the world to me, but I could never burden you with something like that."

"Oh, grandmother, please. It wouldn't be a burden at all. Knowing that you love it so much, it would be my pleasure."

"You know what else is pleasurable my loving grandson? Dating."

I snorted a laugh. "Grandmother—"

"Are you dating anybody?"

I shut my eyes and dropped my head back between my shoulders.

Grandmother was a matchmaker in her youth. Had an office, business cards, and actual clients. Was responsible for a few love connections including that of my parents who were sailing the Atlantic as we spoke. They retired that spring and left New York on a two-year-long excursion they'd embarked on just that month, with no plans of returning on American soil anytime soon.

As happy as my parents were in their thirty-plus years union, I just wished grandmother didn't attempt to achieve the same for me.

"I am dating, actually," I lied.

"Wonderful Bryant, oooh!" she said, excitement laced in her tone. "Is she as great as I think she is? Is she the one?"

"Yup." I squeezed my lids shut and cringed. "And it's serious, too. Can you believe that?"

God, I hope she did.

Relationships were the last thing on my mind. The absolute last thought I had in a day. In fact, I hadn't thought of a relationship until this very moment when my grandmother made me lie to her.

"I can! I absolutely must meet her!"

"Yes, you must. One day grandmother. Some time in the future."

I'd committed my time to money, that was my focus. My commitment to my earning potential was so serious, I had the dollar sign tatted on my left ring finger to prove it.

"One day real soon and in the very near future," my grandmother said next. "I'll be in the city on Saturday for your cousin Addison's final bridal fitting. I can meet the love of your life then."

I gulped the air. "Uh... what?"

"You'll be at Addison's New Year's Eve nuptials, right? In the Hamptons? Of course you will! She told me all about you giving her and her fiancé an early wedding gift by footing a handsome portion of the bill. I'm so thrilled it will be at the Gold Coast castle. That's where that handsome R&B singer and his wife wedded last year, too."

I slid to the edge of my seat. "Yes, grandmother, The Joneses, I know. And yes, I'll be there. Now, about you meeting my girlfriend this weekend—"

"Yes! I'm excited to see her. Oh, I'm sure she is a rare gem if she's caught your eye."

"*Shit,*" I mumbled to myself.

"What's that Bryant?"

"I said, *she* sure is."

I was up and out of my seat, walking my way to my slanted office window to peer out of it. The building and the land it sat on belonged to me. I'd bought the land five years prior and financed the construction of the building I now stood in. Even sectioned out a portion of real estate designated as a public space for employees and visitors to sit out in and enjoy. It was relaxing to see nothing in the distance, and what my eyes fell on belonged to me.

"Great, so Saturday it is! I'm thinking brunch or an early lunch? Oooh! I'm so excited to meet your girlfriend, Bryant, or your potential wife perhaps?"

I inhaled an encouraging breath and on my exhale said, "One step at a time, grandmother."

"I'll tell you what?" she began. "At our meet-up we can discuss the property and you managing it while I get to learn all about your new girlfriend. We can feed two birds with one seed."

I dropped my head forward and pinched the innermost corners of my eyes. "Sounds like a plan."

The moment I ended the call with my grandmother, I dropped myself down onto my leather office chair and grunted.

"What the fuck was that Bryant?!" I scolded. "Where the hell are you going to find a girlfriend you don't even have in time for the weekend?"

The plan for the call was to ease into the land my grandmother had in her possession. Investors offered to pay actual money for the acquisition of that land. I had plans to slip in there an agreement involving my private equity and venture capital firm just to ensure I had a lucrative piece of that pie because it would surely bring in bank. All I had to do was get my grandmother to agree to let me take it off her hands, which I knew she'd do, she'd do anything for the grandson who carried the surname of her husband as his first name. But no, I just had to lie.

"Mr. Greene," I heard from my glass office door.

I swiveled my chair that way to see Emily, a petite blonde with sapphire eyes peering into me from the threshold. She wore a smile that was both seductive and cunning. I recognized the look because I'd seen it tons of times before.

I returned a smile of my own to be polite. "Emily?"

"Oh good, you remember my name." She straightened her posture and poked her breasts out. I arched a brow. "I was just checking in to see if you needed anything."

My eyes moved to the solid gold digital clock on my desk. I'd only arrived at my office half-an-hour earlier. She'd checked in on me about fifteen minutes prior.

"Nope," I said. "As I told you fifteen minutes earlier, I'm fine. But thank you, Emily."

She grinned. "Oh, you can call me Em."

I wrinkled my brows. "I think Emily will do just fine for me, thank you."

Emily was the brand new intern at my company, The Greene Group. The company operated out of the top floor of the 16-story building I owned. Each floor served as the headquarters for my businesses that ranged from my franchise dinner theaters and my private equity and venture capital firm to the glass fabrication and installation company I also owned. I'd recently purchased a waste removal corporation from a business associate desperate to get the failing business off his hands. After adding the company to my business portfolio in the fall, it had shown major growth as I'd expected. I had plans to acquire a few other failing businesses that also showed earning potential. There really was no such thing as having too many streams of income. That's the only way I know how to make money grow.

"Okay," Emily said low. Her tongue licked at her bottom lip slowly and I scoffed a laugh in response. "Well, if you need anything, Mr. Greene, and I do mean anything, please let me know."

I stared at her for a moment and she did the same. Ms. Emily was an aggressive one, the type a man like me had to be careful around.

"Uh-huh," I replied. "Thank you, Emily. That will be all."

She nodded her exit, closing my door behind herself.

I laughed to myself while shaking my head once I was alone again.

This was nothing new. Women and their unsubtle subtleness. It was the first lesson my father taught me when he noticed the sneaker cleaning business I started at 14-years old was taking off and the girls at my prep school were practically throwing themselves at me.

"Son," he said, "it's a wonderful thing to be desired, but you must be careful where you place your attention. Some of those who admire you are looking to destroy you. Don't be too eager to drink from any cup, because it could be poison."

Women were beautiful to me, I loved them. Everything about them. But they were also trouble and distractions. Discipline was a must. I've learned that in this man's world, you're chasing two things - money or women. And when you're chasing one of them the other is getting away. So I chose money. It's loyal and doesn't require much maintenance and reassurance of its worth.

I palmed my cordless office phone and pressed the # symbol to dial up my executive assistant, Chelsea.

Now, Chelsea was a Pitbull in a skirt. I'd be lost without her. She was also a lesbian who couldn't care less about my dick or touching it.

"Good morning, Mr. Greene."

"Good day, Chelsea. How's my calendar for the first half of the day?"

"Clear sir."

"Perfect. Then I will step out to run a few errands," I said. "I need to check on the new dinner theater being built uptown and will be out of the office for the rest of the day."

"Would you like for me to call the car around?"

"Unnecessary," I replied. "I'll drive myself. I need the time to think."

She giggled. "You're the only person I know who finds driving in New York City to be ideal for thinking."

"The chaos is enlightening."

She scoffed a laugh. "Whatever you say, sir."

I smiled.

"I will transfer any important calls to your cell but those that are not time sensitive, I'll just send to your voice mail. Does this work?"

"As always, yes it does."

"Great, enjoy the rest of your day, Mr. Greene."

"I will thank you." I was just about to hang up when I remembered, "Oh, and one other thing, Chels."

"Sir?"

"Emily Warren, the intern that works on my floor in the mornings?"

"Yes, the new girl."

"Please speak with her regarding her conduct while at the office. She seems a bit too eager to please me if you catch my drift."

Chelsea scoffed another laugh. "I know exactly what you mean sir. I'll have a talk with her right now."

"Appreciate it, Chelsea."

"Enjoy your drive, sir."

Chaos was exactly what I needed in that instance. Deciding how I would pull this brunch or lunch off with my grandmother this weekend would take an immense amount of thinking and, if I can be honest, scheming. I couldn't buy my way out of it... or could I?

Either way, it would take a miracle because as I took steps toward my walk-in closet to retrieve my black double-breasted wool coat, I had no idea where I would find a willing participant to not only accompany me to this meet-up with my grandmother but to convincingly pull off being in a relationship with me.

I *needed* that Morgansville property and I was going to get it by any means necessary.

"God help me," I said, as I exited through my office door.

END OF SNEAK PEEK

About the Author

Brookelyn Mosley is a captivating voice in the world of black romance literature. With a gift for weaving heartfelt narratives and steamy encounters, she invites readers on journeys of love, passion, and self-discovery. Through her compelling storytelling, Brookelyn celebrates the beauty of black love and explores the complexities of relationships with authenticity and depth. With over 40+ titles, her stories resonate with true-blue readers, touching hearts and inspiring conversations about love, identity, and resilience.

Connect With Me Online!

Facebook: http://facebook.com/brookelynmosley
Facebook Reading Group: Brookelynites Book Lounge
Instagram: @Brookelynmosley
My Website: BrookelynMosley.com
My Readers Website: BKBookLounge.com
My Mailing List: BK Insiders

www.ingramcontent.com/pod-product-compliance
Lightning Source LLC
Chambersburg PA
CBHW031407310726
48971CB00003B/770